F
PRA

SONORAN
LOVE SONG

SONORAN LOVE SONG

•

Marilyn Prather

AVALON BOOKS
NEW YORK

PRINTED IN THE UNITED STATES OF AMERICA
ON ACID-FREE PAPER
BY HADDON CRAFTSMEN, BLOOMSBURG, PENNSYLVANIA

To June Woodring and Pat Lynch,
fellow writers and friends,
for their priceless words of encouragement
when I needed them most.

Chapter One

The sun was sinking, blood red, behind the low, ragged peaks of the Sierrita Mountains as the Greyhound bus swung into the parking lot of a squat, whitewashed building.

Callie Townsend stared through a dirty window of the bus into the gathering gloom of night. *Hawk's Market*, a neon sign proclaimed in a long pane of glass at the front of the building. Near the door of the market, a huge brown-and-white dog sat on its haunches, its ears back, its eyes trained on the bus.

Other than the portly, middle-aged bus driver and two fellow passengers, the dog was the first sign of life that Callie had seen since Tucson. Unless she counted the almost human forms of the saguaro cacti that stood like silent sentinels everywhere she looked across the bleak landscape.

"Rio Puerco," the driver's voice boomed.

"I must be insane," Callie mumbled under her breath. She gathered her purse and picked up her camera case, which rested on the seat. She trudged down the aisle, past her traveling companions, a young couple—almost kids— with identical blond spiked hairdos and bored expressions on their faces.

A blast of air, hot as a stoked furnace, took Callie's breath away as she emerged from the bus.

1

''Be careful now,'' the driver cautioned. He touched her elbow to help her negotiate the step down to the ground.

Careful. If she'd been careful, she wouldn't have fallen for her aunt Tisha's glowing description of the Sonoran Desert. She would have clearly thought matters through for herself and chosen another destination.

Was she still so shaken over the sudden death of her fiancé, and the grim revelations that had followed in the weeks afterward, that she could no longer make rational decisions?

No, she thought, watching as the bus roared off and she was left alone in the parking lot.

The truth was, in many ways she'd grown stronger since that cold day when the sheriff's deputy had appeared at her door with the news of Nolan's drowning. She'd discovered an inner source of strength that she hadn't known she'd possessed. Yet, during the thirteen months since his death, she'd been reminded of her vulnerability, too. At times she'd fallen into a state of depression so strong, so dark, that she'd moved through each day like a sleepwalker with almost no thought or care as to where she was going. One minute she would rail against the injustices fate had suddenly heaped on her in the person of Nolan Jamison. The next she would break down in tears because she feared she would never again find peace and happiness in her life.

The nightmarish questions persisted. Was Nolan's death a freak accident, as the coroner's report officially stated? Or had he taken his own life because he'd known his charade was about to be exposed?

''You're suffering from what we call post-traumatic stress disorder,'' Dr. Simmons, her physician since her birth twenty-five years ago, had told her the day she'd finally sought his help. ''The shock to your system upon finding out the truth about your fiancé is similar to the trauma experienced by a soldier on a battlefield. It's obvious that the demands of your job are wearing you down too. I recommend that you indulge yourself for once, take a leave of absence from work. A complete change of scenery would be beneficial—someplace that's nice and quiet, where you can lounge in the sun all day.''

Dr. Simmons had smiled and reached over to pat her hand. ''If I might give you one final piece of advice, Callie. As you know, your father and I were friends for many years. If he were here today, I'm certain he'd agree with what I'm about to tell you. Allow yourself the freedom to think about falling in love again. It will help you to heal. In any case, take at least a month off.''

A month. She had accrued that much vacation time at the law firm where she slaved as an overworked and underpaid administrative assistant. But she'd quickly calculated that the funds in her meager savings account would stretch to cover a room at a budget motel and fast food meals for two weeks, tops.

Then, like a guardian angel, Aunt Tisha had intervened. ''A small gift,'' the stylish sixty-something woman had declared, pressing a fat envelope into Callie's palm. ''My portfolio has tripled this past year.''

But the ''small gift'' had come with a string attached.

''For peace and quiet, Callie, you must go to Arizona, to a very special place. Casa de la Rosa Blanca. The House of the White Rose,'' Aunt Tisha had proudly interpreted, inching a glossy brochure into Callie's hand. ''Your uncle Willard and I spent a wildly romantic second honeymoon there.'' Her gray eyes danced with sudden sparks. ''I promise, Callie, that you'll fall in love with the inn. The desert will seduce you, and you won't want to come home.''

I want to go home right now, Callie thought, though she had to admit that the picture of Casa de la Rosa Blanca on the front of the brochure had caught her eye, and the teaser about how the inn had come by its name had piqued her interest. But what about the brochure's glowing description of Rio Puerco as ''a jewel in the desert''? The only jewel Callie saw was in the dome of purple sky above. The evening star winked at her in ruby hues from its dark nest in the heavens as she stooped to pick up the two pieces of luggage the driver had deposited on the gravel. With her purse and the bag that held her precious Nikon camera, she could manage only one of the heavy suitcases.

Who's going to steal them anyway? she asked herself, nervously eyeing the spotted dog who was sulkily tracking her every move from its post. She took a couple of cautious steps toward the market. What would she do if the mongrel decided she didn't belong there?

"Don't be silly," she muttered to herself. "The dog's harmless. Besides, there are lights on in the store, so some-one must be inside."

Just then her throat developed a tickle, and she tried to ease it by swallowing. That only made matters worse, and she started to cough. The dog bared its teeth and glowered at her.

Perspiration beaded on Callie's palms. She gripped the suitcase tighter, afraid the handle might slip from her grasp and provoke an attack by the mongrel.

Dogs can sense fear. Hadn't her father once told her that? Slowly she began to move forward again, hopeful her deliberate pace would convince the snarling beast that she posed no threat.

Her bluff must have worked. The mongrel bared its teeth a second time, then turned and trotted off around the corner of the building.

Releasing a pent-up breath, Callie wiped her hands on her slacks and reached for the handle of the market's front door. No sooner had her fingers curled around the knob than she glimpsed movement in the window of the store. She watched in disbelief as what looked to be a man's large, bony hand swung the cardboard sign from reading *Open* to *Closed*.

Callie tried the door anyway. It was locked. She waved and called in an effort to attract the man's attention, but to no avail.

The neon sign that read *Hawk's Market* suddenly flickered off, and the store was shrouded in darkness. Either whoever was inside was deaf or he was a stickler for closing on time. Or maybe he just didn't care for strangers.

What now? she wondered with dismay. She looked toward the mountains. All that was left of the sunset was a thin band of crimson bleeding over the rims of the bald peaks. A shiver crept up her spine and she clenched her hands tight until her fingernails bit painfully into the flesh of her palms.

I am not going to have a panic attack, she told herself. She hadn't come this far only to cower and cave in to fear because her plans weren't working out as she'd expected. Her aunt had taken care of the reservations for her trip and had assured her just the week before that ''someone from the inn will be there to meet you, dear.''

But what if the innkeepers had gotten the dates wrong? Maybe they were under the mistaken impression that the guest from Milwaukee was due in the next day. Or even the next week.

She made herself take a couple of slow, deliberate breaths and attempted to order her thoughts. Her first priority, she decided, was to locate a pay phone and call the inn.

Callie squinted into the near-darkness. There was no pay phone in sight, only a jumble of crates stacked against one side of the building. It occurred to her that maybe there was no such thing as a phone in Rio Puerco—or no other inhabitants except for the unsociable person who had refused her entry into his store.

And the person's dog, Callie was reminded as a low, ominous growl sent more shivers racing along her nerves.

A fresh wave of fear gripped Callie as the dog crouched low and edged toward her. Heart pounding, she looked for something—anything—she could use as a weapon against the mongrel. She spotted a club-size piece of wood on the ground and made a desperate grab for it.

In the next instant the sound of tires spinning on gravel

arrested her attention, and she froze in place as a pair of headlights blinded her. Momentarily forgetting the threat from the mongrel, she dropped the board and shielded her eyes with her hands.

"Miss Townsend?" a deep, resonant voice demanded.

Callie lowered her hands. Through the glare she saw first the shape of a truck or van, then the form of a man walking toward her.

"Well?" he said, covering the distance between them in several long strides.

Outlined in the headlights, the man looked impossibly tall, his face hidden in shadows. "I'm C-Callie Townsend," she stammered. "Are you—"

"Reece Tanner," he interrupted.

"The driver from Casa de la Rosa Blanca," she finished, uncertain whether she wouldn't rather take her chances with the surly hound than this man whose eyes glowed like embers in the dark outline of his face.

"The manager of Casa de la Rosa Blanca."

"But—" Callie felt confused. Hadn't the brochure listed Henry and Corrine Bennett as proprietors? Now this stranger was telling her that he was in charge.

She caught a glimpse of granitelike jaw and firm, generous mouth as Reece Tanner moved a step closer. Her tongue flicked over her lips to moisten them. "Is this how you greet all your guests, Mr. Tanner, blinding them with your headlights?"

"Just the ones I have to pick up in the dark," he replied evenly.

Callie bristled. "It wasn't dark when I got here." She'd never been to such a place before where in the blink of an eye it turned from day into night.

"Then the bus was early. Are we going to stand around arguing the point," he went on in a softer tone, "or are you going to get in the van?"

Callie's anger deflated as fast as a punctured balloon. What choice did she have? He had her reservation, not to mention the money for her month's room and board. She had three pieces of luggage and nowhere else to spend the night. "Would you mind—"

"I wouldn't," he said, hefting the two heavy cases in his hands as if they were lunch boxes. "Coming, Miss Townsend?"

Callie had taken no more than a couple of steps when a throaty growl menaced her from behind. "Help!" she cried as a streak of fur came racing at her heels.

All at once Reece Tanner was nearby. He stepped easily between her and the dog. "Down, Chico!" he commanded.

To Callie's astonishment, the mongrel dropped to the ground, put its head between its paws, and whimpered. To her even greater astonishment, Reece Tanner knelt beside the dog and began to rub it behind the ears.

"All right, boy," Reece said in a gentle voice. "You've got to promise to mind your manners from now on."

Chico gave an excited yip and thumped his tail against the ground. Then, with a pat on the rump from Reece, the dog meekly lumbered away.

A shaky laugh escaped Callie. "That was amazing, Mr. Tanner."

He rose and put his hands on his hips. "Not particularly. It just takes the right touch."

Her gaze went to his hands. Even in shadow they looked capable and strong. All at once she realized that, except for her knees quaking like leaves in a fierce wind, she felt normal again; the sense of panic was gone. She glanced toward the market, half expecting the owner to show his face and demand to know what the commotion was about.

"Mr. Hawk isn't, um, afraid that something might happen to his dog—to Chico—letting him roam at night?"

Reece Tanner chuckled. "I think I'm safe in saying that Ada Hawk isn't afraid of anything. Or anyone, for that matter. As for Chico, he isn't apt to roam anywhere that Ada doesn't want him to."

So the owner of Hawk's Market was a woman, and one who, Callie surmised, did just as she pleased.

"Now that the danger's passed, Miss Townsend, are you ready to go?"

She saw Reece Tanner clearly for the first time since they'd met. Trapped in the naked glow of the headlights, his body, clad in jeans and a plain white shirt that was open at the neck, appeared tough and spare and sinewy. Her gaze traveled up to rest on a broodingly handsome face topped by a swath of unruly hair the color of midnight.

There was an aura of virility about this man that both intrigued and unnerved her. His eyes assessed hers for the length of a heartbeat, and she began to suspect that she looked like some prey the cat had carried home, roughed-up and disheveled from her long trip and her jittery encounter with Chico. Her makeup would have worn off hours ago, and her hair—the color and length of a shock of ripe wheat, according to Aunt Tisha's dramatic description of it—was coming loose in stray wisps from the French braid she'd fashioned early that day.

Reece held open the passenger door of the van for her. She had a choice to make—sit in the front with him or pile onto the bench seat located behind the driver's seat. She decided on the bench.

The vehicle, from what she could tell in the dark, had seen better days. The engine sputtered and choked when Reece stepped on the gas, leaving Callie with the impression that it might die altogether before they got out of the parking lot. Then, to make matters worse, the tickling started again in Callie's throat.

"I . . . You wouldn't happen to have a cough drop or a mint, would you?" she asked the back of Reece Tanner's head.

"Sure don't," he said in a casual tone that made her think maybe he cared more about dogs than people.

But when the tickle erupted into a fit of coughing, Reece swung the van back toward the market and hit the brakes.

He reached around to unlatch the side door. "Come on," he said. "You're about to meet Ada."

Before she could mount a protest, Reece was out of the van and pacing up to the front door of the market.

"Ada!" he called, rapping on the door.

Callie's protest of "Really, I'm fine," was followed by another bout of coughing.

"Doesn't sound like it to me," Reece said with a second hard rap on the door. His head pivoted in her direction. "Don't worry. Ada's been watching us all along."

The question on the tip of Callie's tongue was thwarted when the door suddenly opened. Lights flashed on inside, illuminating the tall, skeletal figure of a woman whose wiry white hair stuck out at odd angles from her head.

"What d'ya want, Reece Tanner?" the woman grumbled. "Can't ya see I'm closed? Or did some of them chips from those boulders of yours finally blind ya?"

"The lady here needs a drink to soothe her throat," he replied in an appeasing tone.

Small, sharp eyes peered out from a face mapped with leathery lines. They looked past Reece to Callie. As if by magic, Callie quit coughing.

"Appears fine to me." Ada harrumphed. But she swung the door wider. "Beverages are in the rear," she said with a flick of her hand. "Beer and soda on the left, juice and milk on the right. You pay in the front."

The store had several narrow aisles of shelves that stretched from floor to ceiling. Without sparing a glance at Reece, Callie sped down one of the aisles. Bypassing the more nutritious juices, she opted for a bottle of old-fashioned cream soda and headed to where Ada stood with her elbows on the counter.

Hawk's Market was strictly no-frills, Callie noticed as Ada rang up the fifty-cent charge on a manual cash register. Callie found herself warming to Ada, despite the woman's gruff manner. She handed over the correct change and looked around for Reece.

"He's gone outside, missy," Ada said, producing a bottle opener from under the counter. "One of the best-looking men I've ever laid eyes on." She popped the top off the cream soda. "And one of the loneliest, I reckon." Her gaze settled on Callie.

Callie stared at the bead of moisture forming on the lip of the brown soda bottle. "Have you known him very long?"

Ada snorted. "Long enough, I suppose. He blew into town five years ago. By himself. No wife or kids. Said he was lookin' for the inn out by the mining town of Vulture's Creek. Next thing ya know, he up and had a job there, working for the Bennetts. Ya stayin' there?"

Callie took a swallow of the cream soda. It tasted sweet and smooth, but there was a strange bite to it when it passed down her throat. "Yes. My aunt and uncle spent their second honeymoon at Casa de la Rosa Blanca." She didn't recall Aunt Tisha saying anything about a mining town.

"The locals have a story to tell about that place. Some tale about young lovers caught up in a big feud, the fellow a *campesino*—that's peasant to you—from south of the border, the girl the daughter of a cattle baron." Ada rested her bony chin on a callused palm. "Ain't never put much stock in such nonsense. But if ya do, I expect you'll be disappointed. Ain't nothin' much out there but mesquite and greasewood and dust. And Reece Tanner. Course, havin' him in your sights for a spell could raise a romantic notion or two." Her mouth split open in a grin.

Callie's fingers tightened around the bottle. "Are there many guests at the inn now?"

"You're the first one in weeks. Not countin' Carlos Aguilar. He's not a tourist, though. Been around these parts so long he's beginnin' to howl at the moon. Hired himself out to the Bennetts some years ago." Ada leaned forward. "Ya'd better get goin', missy, or Reece might leave ya behind."

"I could always stay someplace else."

Ada hooted a laugh. ''I was just kiddin' ya. Reece ain't that kind of man. Besides, there's no place else to stay unless you're itchin' for the company of ghosts at Vulture's Creek.''

Callie thanked Ada and left, wondering just what kind of man Reece Tanner was besides a handsome and lonely one who had the power to soothe savage beasts.

The trip to the inn gave Callie plenty of time for contemplation. The highway stretched ahead of the van like a ribbon frosted silver by the moon, while a raspy male voice belted out a song of love and heartbreak from the vehicle's radio. The plaintive tune seemed as suited to the lonely landscape of Callie's heart as it did to the flat lay of the desert and the black hills framed in the distance.

She wondered if Reece had turned on the country-and-western station to deflect any need for conversation. At least he'd apologized for the van's lack of a working air conditioner, with the assurance that it would be fixed the next day.

''Usually the temperature dips at night,'' he'd said, ''but this year the weather's been strange.''

Then he'd switched on a small fan that was mounted on the dashboard, sending a blast of warm air toward the backseat.

Images of home careened through Callie's head as the van rolled down the highway—a collage of hues and sounds and scents she associated with her aunt's cozy house outside of Milwaukee where she'd stayed for seven years after her parents' divorce and her mother's remarriage. Though she had her own apartment now, she considered whether she would have been smarter to pitch a tent in the lush green meadow bordering her aunt's backyard and camp there for a month rather than venture over a thousand miles searching for peace in the middle of the desert.

Once she wouldn't have questioned her decision. She would have just gone with her instincts. That was BNJ—Before Nolan Jamison. This was After Nolan Jamison.

"SNOR," the announcer's voice crackled over the radio, "cactus-land's home to the greatest names in contemporary and classic country music. All hits, all the time, twenty-four hours a day." A guitar riff introduced a female contralto delivering a bouncy song about "dancin' and romancin' in my sweet brown-eyed baby's arms."

The tune came to a rousing conclusion just as Callie downed the last of the cream soda and Reece Tanner made an abrupt turn onto an unpaved road. The lip of the bottle hit her mouth, narrowly avoiding a collision with her front teeth.

The van bumped and rocked along for an endless distance before Callie spied any hint of civilization—a pinpoint of light pulsing on the horizon like a star fallen from heaven.

She leaned forward. "Is that the inn?" she shouted over the noise from the radio.

"That's it," Reece confirmed. He jabbed a button on the dashboard, and the barrage of tunes about dancin' and romancin' and hearts that needed mendin' was silenced.

Fixing her eyes on the spot of light beyond the shadowy shape of Reece Tanner's head, Callie had the eerie notion that she was being escorted to the last outpost on earth.

"It seems like we're moving but not getting anywhere," she remarked.

Reece laughed. "Out here distances are deceptive. Things aren't always what they first appear to be."

"You mean like a mirage?"

"In some cases." He made a quick gesture with his hand. "The light you see is real enough. But it's much farther away than you might judge. That's because the topography of the land is mostly flat as a board, the air clear as a bell. There's nothing to clutter the vision, obstruct the view."

Things aren't always what they first appear to be. She was tempted to tell him that what was true of the Sonoran Desert could be said of people too.

"Do you like living out here?" she couldn't help asking.

"Do I like living out here?" he echoed.

An eternity seemed to pass before he spoke again. "I've gotten used to it," he said.

For a man who, according to Ada, had come looking for the inn and taken a job there, he didn't sound very enthused. Curiosity made her ask, "Where are you from?"

"Here, there, and everywhere," he replied in a clipped tone.

A drifter of sorts, she guessed, sizing him up, *who doesn't like being asked questions about himself*.

The van sped on toward the light. Finally Callie saw the irregular shape of a building ahead. A few minutes later, Reece swung the van into a drive that formed a large semicircle in front of the two-story lodge.

Post lanterns illuminated a large sign that read *Casa de la Rosa Blanca*. The lamps cast a weak, pale glow across Callie's path as she followed Reece up a walkway of crushed stones. But the row of darkened windows on the second floor of the inn seemed to send her a cold greeting, and a statue stationed by the entrance gazed at her with sightless eyes.

As if the manager of the uninviting-looking inn had uttered a secret password, the massive front door creaked open. Reece turned toward Callie. Except for the dark stubble that graced his jaw, the barest movement of a muscle in his creek, his face bore the same closed expression as the statue.

"One of the best-looking men I've ever big eyes on." Callie's gaze locked with his, and she had to agree with Ada's assessment of Reece Tanner. Yet Ada had also declared him to be one of the loneliest. *Why?* The question echoed in Callie's mind until she imagined he could hear it.

"Welcome to the House of the White Rose," he said with a slight smile. But his eyes were veiled in shadow.

Chapter Two

Callie stepped over the threshold and into a cavernous lobby that was lit mostly by candlelight. A rush of refrigerated air cooled her cheeks. The uplifting notes of an aria floated soothingly around her. The flames of the candles seemed to move in time to the music, throwing shadows up the high walls and into the room's mysterious dark corners.

On the far side of the lobby, a fire burned in a huge stone hearth. Near the hearth, a grouping of rough-hewn sofas and chairs held court. Shelves overflowing with books occupied one entire wall from floor to ceiling.

Framed paintings adorned the other walls. As Callie's eyes adjusted to the dimly lit room, she noticed that most of the paintings were of desert scenes. But one stood out as different—a rendering of a single long-stemmed white rose set against a background of velvety blackness. Arrested by the painting's lifelike beauty, she turned to make a comment to Reece. To her surprise he was gone, vanished like a phantom in the dark.

"Ah, so you've arrived safely."

Callie wheeled around and nearly collided with a short, heavyset Hispanic woman. Though she judged the woman to be only a little younger than Ada Hawk, her appearance was as soft as Ada's was hard, and her eyes sparkled with warmth.

"I'm Elena," she said, "and I'll be seeing to your comfort, Miss Townsend, during your stay with us at Casa de la Rosa Blanca." The name of the inn flowed from the woman's lips like a charmed melody.

"Mr. Tanner has taken your luggage upstairs," she went on. "Come. I'll show you to your room."

Callie wondered how he could have moved past her without her being aware of it. Maybe it was because she'd been so captivated by the painting of the white rose. She followed Elena to a staircase at the far end of the room. Electric lamps in wrought-iron holders lit the way up the wide, winding steps.

At the top of the stairs there was a balcony, with a corridor leading to the left. On the right was a blind corner. Halfway down the corridor, light spilled from an open doorway. All the rest of the doors were closed.

Callie saw no sign of Reece as Elena led her to the open doorway. A fat white wax candle burned in a wall sconce just inside the room; shadows cast by its flame danced across the gleaming wood floor and up the sand-colored walls.

The room was altogether charming, Callie decided. Vivid splashes of turquoise and pink and mauve graced the tasseled throw that covered the heavy oak bed and the tieback curtains that hung on either side of the long double windows. A night table with an ornately shaded electric lamp stood at one side of the bed, and a brass-framed mirror occupied a corner of the room. The smell of candle smoke faintly scented the air.

"Here is your luggage," Elena said.

Callie's two suitcases sat at the foot of the bed. Elena took one of the cases and placed it near a massive bureau. Then she went to the windows and cranked open the shutters. "So you can admire the view of our courtyard. And the moon." She turned to Callie. "It is said that the moon shines more brightly in the Sonoran than anywhere else in

God's creation.'' She smiled. "You're from *Milwaukee,* Miss Townsend?''

The housekeeper made it sound as if Milwaukee were a foreign country. "I live near the city—in a suburb," Callie replied.

"Then you will be amazed at how many stars you'll see in our night sky. Now''—Elena clasped her hands together over her blue embroidered dress—"to more practical matters. I'll bring you some dinner.''

Callie hadn't thought about eating or food, a habit that had become too common of late. "I had a sandwich at the airport in Tucson."

"Only a sandwich? No wonder you are so . . . slender.'' Elena raised a finely arched brow. "Well, I have freshly made gazpacho—cold soup—in the kitchen. It's a favorite of Mr. Tanner's," she added, as if that were proof enough of its worth.

"All right," Callie agreed, "but just a small bowl, please.'' She glanced around the room. "Have you worked at the inn very long, Elena?''

"Eighteen years.''

"My aunt and uncle spent their second honeymoon here. The Bennetts were owners at the time.''

Elena nodded. "They still are the owners. Mr. Bennett was in failing health for a great while. Finally they asked Mr. Tanner to manage the inn. The Bennetts are gone now to California, where his sister lives, so that he may receive special medical treatment. They're not sure when they will be coming back. Maybe in the spring. Maybe later.''

"How many guests are here now?''

"Just you.'' The housekeeper smiled. "We do get a bit more business in the winter—regulars who return every year. We hire on a few workers then, too, for several months. But the Bennetts have made their money on the inn and are not interested in making too many improvements. They prefer to leave things pretty much as they are. Well, I'll get the soup now and bring you extra linens.''

Left to her own devices, Callie set her travel bag on the bed. She unzipped the camera case and inspected her Nikon for any sign of damage. When she was satisfied the camera had survived the trip intact, she placed it back in the case and put the case in the top drawer of the bureau.

Elena returned and Callie ate the chilled, spicy soup while the housekeeper put the fresh linens in the bathroom. Before she left, she advised Callie to leave the candle burning.

"That way you'll have a source of light after you turn off the lamp and the moon is too low to shine in."

Candlelight and moonlight and a painting of a white rose, thought Callie as she eased her body into a tub of warm rose petal–scented bathwater.

This moment is the beginning of my vacation, she told herself. *From now on until I leave Casa de la Rosa Blanca, I will follow Dr. Simmons's orders,* she vowed.

After a long soak, Callie wrapped herself in one of the thick towels and washed off the remnants of her makeup in front of the sink. Then she unpacked her clothes and took out her white satin gown and matching robe. The set had been a gift from Aunt Tisha, along with an envelope containing a bit of mad money "to spend on whatever you please, dear," Tisha had said.

She slid the gown over her head and drew on the robe, cinching it at the waist. After a quick rummage in her travel bag, she found her hairbrush.

She eyed her reflection critically in the mirror—the straight nose, inherited from her father; the high cheekbones that she considered her one good feature; the mouth, a little too wide in proportion to the rest of her face, yet a perfect copy of her mother's.

She brushed her hair until it fell in loose waves over her shoulders and the silky fabric of her robe.

I should've had it cut before I left home. Something in her had rebelled at the idea, and so she'd left it long. Was it because Nolan had made it clear that he wanted her to have it cropped short in a chic, above-the-chin style?

A familiar feeling of tightness suddenly gripped her chest, radiating outward from the center as if a giant were slowly grinding his foot into her breastbone.

She shivered and clutched her robe shut where it exposed her flesh. She gave a soft groan as the brush dropped with a clatter onto the floor from fingers that had suddenly grown numb and cold. For the second time that evening she wondered if she were about to have a panic attack. At least she knew she wasn't dying. Or slowly going crazy.

Dr. Simmons had diagnosed the attacks after she'd experienced the feeling that she was finally losing her grip on her sanity while waiting in the grocery checkout line one afternoon. Only then had she realized the attack had come two weeks to the day after she'd stood in the blustery cold and watched Nolan's casket being lowered into the frozen ground at Maple Lawn Cemetery.

She'd declined Dr. Simmons's offer of medication to help control the attacks, hoping that the incident was a fluke. She'd had another attack the very next day—and the day after that and the day after that. At Dr. Simmons's urging, she'd finally joined a support group.

Gradually she'd learned ways to lessen the effects of the attacks, then to thwart them altogether. She'd even begun to keep a journal where, in writing, she poured out her anger, the feelings of disillusionment and abandonment that she couldn't bring herself to fully share even with the caring members of her support group. She'd dabbled in writing poetry and discovered that the lines she scribbled down in short, furious bursts reflected the strange, exotic images she'd been capturing on film.

She'd even gotten the courage to enter several of her photographs in a contest sponsored by the prestigious Graham Gallery in Milwaukee. One of them—a candid black-and-white of an elderly man sitting on a park bench on a snowy day—had taken Best of Show.

Gunther Graham, the owner of the gallery, had asked to see other examples of her work. She'd whipped together a small portfolio. He'd been impressed. "Call me," he'd said, "when you return from your vacation. We might have room for a few of your photographs in our winter exhibit."

She'd celebrated his positive response to her work with visions of one day realizing her secret dream of having her work on display in other galleries, of gaining a name for herself as a serious photographer. She'd celebrated, too, her eleventh week of freedom from the dreaded panic attacks.

I'm not going to let a passing thought about Nolan trigger one now, she told herself. She concentrated on taking slow, deep breaths and began to count backward from ten in her head. She'd discovered that the mental exercise was helpful in diverting her attention away from an impending attack.

The sensation of tightness in her chest abated and the feeling came back in her fingers. But she still felt cold, and her hands shook slightly as she stooped to pick up the brush and lay it on top of the bureau.

Crossing the room, she turned off the lamp but left the candle burning, as Elena had suggested. There was just enough light for her to make her way to the windows.

Callie looked out and stifled a surprised gasp at the odd sight of a sculpture garden in the courtyard below. In the center of the garden, a two-tiered fountain thrust a misty spray of water high into the air.

She opened the window a crack and heard the soft splashing of the water cascading into the lower bowl of the fountain. She detected an undercurrent of music in the sound. At first she thought it was her imagination or the strains of another classical selection drifting up from the lower regions of the inn. But the sensual melody was played on a single instrument—a guitar. The tune brought back poignant memories of the times when her father strummed folk songs in the evenings on the swing in their backyard. She'd loved to hear him play, and he'd promised her he'd teach her how to chord. Then something had gone terribly wrong in her parents' marriage. Within six months her mother had asked for a divorce and Callie's life was turned upside down.

"Your father's a poet—and a dreamer," her mother used to say, with a critical edge to her voice. She'd set narrowed brown eyes on Callie. *"You're too much like him. If you knew what's good for you, you'd be a pragmatist like me and quit that silly, sentimental daydreaming."*

Her mother had been right. *As always,* Callie thought now, closing her eyes. But she'd never succeeded in purging her sentimental streak. And now the dreamer in her was responding to the music drifting over the moonlit desert night. She slipped into her pair of sandals and went downstairs. A few candles were still burning in the lobby, and Callie saw their glow reflected in a set of double doors at the far end of the room. She opened one of the doors and discovered that it led to the courtyard.

The temperature outside had dropped slightly, and a mild breeze blew through the yard, buffeting Callie's cheeks with tiny pearls of water from the fountain. The music came to an abrupt conclusion. There was no other sound except for the tinkling melody of the fountain, and no one about, except for the statues standing like paper-white ghosts under a full moon.

Callie began to stroll among the statues, struck by the fact that they were all grouped in pairs. Her attention was arrested by the perfectly chiseled forms of what were so obviously couples. But was it a trick of light that distorted their faces into expressions of agony and longing?

She paused to touch the sculpted arm of a handsome male figure, then pressed her palm and fingers flat to the cool, alabaster hand of his lovely female companion. She was both fascinated and somehow disturbed to find that her hand was a perfect match to the statue's. At the same time her mind was at work, scrutinizing the garden with a practiced eye, imagining how the stone couple might look through the lens of her Nikon with the first blush of day tinting their pale torsos, or the noon sun bleaching their faces with its white-hot rays.

She walked around the pair in order to view the couple from a fresh perspective. Backing away a few steps, she collided all at once with another statue. She started to turn and struck her foot against something—perhaps a rock. Set off balance, she made a desperate grab for the statue's arm, and missed.

Two other arms caught hold of her—arms of flesh, not lifeless stone.

"Steady," a masculine voice said.

Callie whirled around and found herself locked in Reece Tanner's embrace. At first she was stunned, aware only of the fact that he was there and had kept her from falling. Then slowly she became conscious of the warmth enfolding her, the clean scent of his skin and slightly rough texture of his shirt pressed against her cheek.

For a fleeting second she experienced a feeling of tranquillity that she hadn't known since before Nolan's death. And something deeper—a thrill of excitement that swept through her veins and quickened her blood. She looked up. Did she only imagine she saw the same conflict of emotions in the dark depths of his eyes? Above the broad brow, his hair gleamed like black satin in the moonlight. No stone statue, she realized, could hope to imitate his potent masculinity or the possessively tender way he was holding her in his arms.

All too soon it was over, and he slid his hands from around her waist to lightly grasp her wrists. Then he released her entirely. "Are you all right?" he asked, looking away.

"Yes, I—" Suddenly she was conscious of her attire— and of the fact that she was trembling, shaken by the intensity of her response to his nearness. "For a moment," she said with a little laugh, "I thought you were a statue."

"For a moment," he said, not laughing, "I thought you were an angel."

She gazed down but sensed he was watching her. "I was looking out my window, admiring the courtyard. I heard music and—"

"That was the 'Sonoran Love Song.' "

She thought he was joking. A glance at his face told her that he was not. He turned to the pair of statues, and she followed the sweep of his hand. "Romeo and Juliet," he said.

Callie stared at the statues, but her mind was on Reece and the "Sonoran Love Song." She wondered if he'd been the musician.

He moved on. "Hugo and Drouet."

She came up beside him. The pair of statues conveyed a feeling of abandonment. "Who are Hugo and Drouet?"

"Victor Hugo, the French writer, and Juliette Drouet, an actress who wrote passionate love letters to him for more than fifty years."

"They never married?"

"No. Now over here . . ." He strode across the courtyard and she followed. "We have Honoré de Balzac, another French writer, by the way, and Evelina Hanska, a Polish countess."

"What's their story?"

"The countess was married to an older man when she met Balzac." He traced the curve of the countess's chin with long, tapered fingers. "Out of respect for the countess's husband, they postponed any involvement until her husband died."

Reece's hands, frosted white by the moonlight, reminded her of an artist's hands, sensitive yet strong. She tore her gaze from him. "That was an honorable thing to do," she said.

Reece gave a short, contemptuous laugh. "It might have been if Balzac hadn't died suddenly after their wedding."

Her glance touched his. "How do you know so much about star-crossed lovers?"

"Because I've made a close study of the subject." He moved a step closer, and she remembered the warmth of his embrace, the comfort of his touch. But his eyes were hidden from her, and the warmth she imagined was gone, replaced by a chill that made her shiver.

"You're cold," he said. He turned so that the moon illumined his face. His gaze raked over her. "You shouldn't be out here in that thin outfit." A muscle in his jaw twitched. "You'd better go inside now."

Her cheeks flamed with embarrassment, and she clutched her robe shut. "Sorry to have taken up your time when you've got more important things to do," she said stiffly.

"No need to apologize," she heard him call after her. "You didn't take up my time, and I don't have more important things to do."

Minutes later, nestled between the cool sheets of her bed, Callie watched the moon trace slanted silver lines across the floor and thought about Reece Tanner. She felt more troubled than she wanted to admit by her encounter with him in the courtyard.

"The desert will seduce you," her aunt had said, *"and you won't want to come home."*

Callie was still skeptical of that; she was less certain of her ability to resist the ardent charms of Reece Tanner. It seemed to her now that Nolan's most ardent caresses paled in comparison to the merest touch from this man she barely knew.

"I've gone over the edge," she muttered to herself.

Not two weeks ago she'd summarily dismissed Dr. Simmons's advice that she allow herself the freedom to fall in love again. She'd told herself she didn't need that kind of freedom, not when she had a tenuous hold on her emotions at best and her life was in a state of flux. Her mind and heart resisted the idea of even casual dating, let alone a serious relationship.

Now here she was in the middle of the desert, without her aunt's sage wisdom and wit to guide her, troubled to the core by her attraction to a virtual stranger, an apparent loner who seemed more at ease telling her about statues of star-crossed lovers than about himself. If she were smart, she'd pack her bags in the morning and board the first bus back to the airport.

But the notion of running away left a sour taste in her mouth. Besides, did she really want to go home? She could see herself moping around her apartment for the rest of the month, alone, wishing Aunt Tisha were there to keep her company. Three days before her departure for Arizona, she'd gotten a breathless phone call from her aunt.

"You'll never guess who phoned, Callie. I lifted the receiver and—can you imagine—there was Beatrice Coleman on the other end! She begged me to come to Paris for a visit. So I've booked a flight for tomorrow."

Callie sighed. Her aunt was thousands of miles away and could be gone for weeks yet. Callie recalled her own determination to flesh out her slender portfolio with some spectacular photographs of the Sonoran Desert. She thought of Vulture's Creek. The ghost town sounded like an answer to a prayer, one that was too good to pass up.

The dreamer in her had made her think for a moment that Reece's embrace, his smoldering gaze, his parting words to her were proof that her feelings for him were mutual. Yet, in the quiet, she could almost hear her mother's sharp voice from the past harping at her for being frivolous and sentimental.

So she told herself that Reece's only concern for her had been to save her from the humiliation of falling flat on her face. But when she finally began to doze off, it was with the haunting melody of the "Sonoran Love Song" playing in her head and an image of Reece Tanner standing amid his forest of lifeless statues burning in her mind. And her last thought was to wonder what twist of fate had brought him to Casa de la Rosa Blanca in the first place.

Callie woke to a blinding stream of light that was directed squarely at her eyes. For an instant she believed the glare came from the headlights of a car. Then she realized that it was the sun shining through the window.

Blinking the sleep from her eyes, she pushed back the covers and swung her legs over the side of the bed. She looked at her watch. Nine o'clock. It had been ages since she'd allowed herself to sleep in that late. The twisted sheets were mute evidence of a restless night, and she recalled that Reece Tanner had been the last thing on her mind as she'd drifted off.

Had she only dreamed of a sculpture garden in the courtyard below and that Reece had held her in his arms?

She went to the window. The sculptures were real, all right. Gazing down, Callie had the bizarre notion that once they had been human too, trapped by fate in this desolate place and slowly scorched by the sun until they turned to lifeless stone.

Maybe I'll become one of them if I stay long enough.

Unnerved by the thought, she turned away from the window. In the quietness, her stomach gave a sudden loud growl, evidence of her need for food and that, for the present at least, she could count herself among the living.

She pulled on a pair of jeans and a red sleeveless top. After whisking her hair into a loose twist at the back of her head and brushing on a bit of blusher and lipstick, she went downstairs in search of breakfast.

In daylight, the lobby, with its faded furnishings and hearth full of dead ashes, looked slightly shabby. Callie discovered a door opposite the ones that led out to the courtyard. This new door stood ajar; she walked through it and found herself in the dining room.

A dozen or more tables dressed with white linen cloths appeared to be waiting for a horde of hungry diners. But the lacquered pine chairs were empty, and only one of the tables sported a place setting of knife, spoon, fork, and crystal water glass. The table was beside a window that looked out on the courtyard.

"Hello!" she called out. There was no response, so she tried again.

"Oh, Miss Townsend, there you are!"

Elena came hustling through a swinging door at the rear of the dining room. "I've waited breakfast for you." With a flutter of her hand, she directed Callie to the table with the silverware.

The housekeeper was like a welcome ray of sunshine in the sedate room as she bustled back and forth from the kitchen, serving Callie a wedge of fresh melon, followed by bacon and French toast with real maple syrup.

Callie ate her meal in a leisurely fashion, her glance wandering to the view of the statues of Romeo and Juliet. The food was very good, and when she finished, she lingered over a second cup of coffee.

"Will there be anything else, Miss Townsend?"

Callie looked up. "Nothing, thank you, Elena, except . . . Is Vulture's Creek far from here?"

Elena snatched Callie's empty plate and the silverware from the table. "How did you learn about Vulture's Creek?"

"From Ada Hawk. She mentioned that the town had once been a mining camp."

"You're not thinking of going there, are you?"

"Yes, I am. Could you give me directions?"

Elena's brow furrowed. "I wouldn't advise visiting Vulture's Creek alone. Perhaps Mr. Tanner could arrange to take you there."

Callie took a swallow of coffee. "I imagine he's—" She started to say too busy, then thought better of it. "I doubt he'd be interested in arranging a tour."

"I would not say so. Besides . . ." Elena fidgeted with the hem of her apron. "Well, a man died at the ghost town.

It was a year ago that Mr. Tanner came across the body just inside the old mine shaft.'' She shook her head. ''The poor man had no identification on him, so the sheriff was called up from Nogales to investigate. It was determined that the man died of natural causes, that there was no foul play. It's believed that he was a vagrant who had taken up residence in one of the old buildings. Money was collected in town to give him a decent burial and he was put to his final rest in the cemetery at Vulture's Creek. Wouldn't you agree, Miss Townsend, that it is sad for one to be all alone in the world?''

Callie's glance was drawn to the courtyard and the sorrowful faces of the doomed lovers. ''Very sad,'' she agreed softly.

Callie left the table without finishing her cup of coffee and headed out to the courtyard. A wave of heat assaulted her face, threatening to cut off her breath, and she was forced to retreat under a roof that shaded a porch skirting a portion of the inn. A row of windows looked out on the courtyard, but the curtains were drawn tight, giving nothing away.

At last a breeze stirred the air, coaxing Callie from the shelter of the porch to walk among the statues. She touched Romeo's sculpted chest. The smooth alabaster was warm against her skin, almost like human flesh. But beneath the sun-glazed surface, she knew, lay only cold stone.

She moved on past the fountain to the back of the yard and was pleasantly surprised to find a botanical garden of saguaro and other cacti. Too late she saw Reece standing in front of a strange-looking plant whose trunk branched out wildly in long, skinny stems. Reece held a shovel in his hand; a small pile of dirt was heaped beside him on the ground.

Callie started to turn back. At that instant Reece glanced over at her and motioned for her to join him.

The way his hair curled damply against the tanned column of his neck, and the straining of his muscles against the fabric of his T-shirt, provoked in her the memory of that moment when he had caught her in his arms.

"So what's your opinion of an ocotillo?" he said, wiping his brow.

"Is that what it is?" Callie stared at the plant, aware that Reece had stepped back to stand beside her. "I'd say it looks more like a dead upside-down octopus."

He gave a short laugh and leaned his arm on the handle of the hoe. "It's not an octopus—or a cactus. The fancy name for it is *Fouguieria,* but I prefer to think of it as a sunrise with thorns."

"A sunrise with thorns?"

His brief smile revealed two rows of flawless white teeth. "In the spring the branches bear blossoms that are about the color of a desert sunrise, but those branches carry some wicked thorns too. Like a lot of things in the desert, the ocotillo is both pretty and dangerous." He wrapped his hand around the hoe. "I'd advise you to keep a safe distance from an ocotillo."

Or maybe I should just keep a safe distance from you, she thought.

"There are a couple of hammocks strung up among the cottonwoods," he went on, pointing toward the oasis. "Before you ask, there's no swimming pool or tennis courts."

Who's asking? "Okay, then I'll laze in a hammock."

"Or you can laze in the spa that we installed last year. You'll find it among the trees too."

"What about Vulture's Creek?"

He looked toward the mountains. "What about it?"

"I'd like to see the town. How do I get there?"

"You're going to strike out dressed like that?" His gaze roved over her. "First off, you'd better get a hat for protection. And something to protect that pretty pale complexion. Hmm . . ." A smile twisted one corner of his mouth. "Those bare toes'll make easy prey for some scorpion. Of course, you're apt to run across a few rattlers, not to mention tarantulas as big as saucers."

Callie locked her arms over her chest. "For your information, I have sunblock—SPF forty, no less—and sensible walking shoes that are so ugly they'll scare off the most fearsome tarantula. And if you think I'm some mindless twit who doesn't—"

"I don't think that at all," he interrupted, though not unkindly. "What I do think is that you're uptight and accustomed to the fast pace of city life. Why don't you go recline in one of those hammocks and cool off for a while."

"And what I think *you* need to do," she shot back, "is to keep your opinions to yourself and start acting like a civil host. And for starters, you could offer your guest a tour of Vulture's Creek. Then maybe . . . just maybe . . ." She spluttered, drew a deep breath, and tried again. "Then maybe your guest wouldn't be so uptight!"

He moved past her and rammed the shovel into the ground. The blade of the shovel missed beheading the ocotillo by a couple of inches—no more. "If you wanted tours and fancier digs," he said with a grunt, "then you should have booked a room at an upscale resort in Tucson or Phoenix."

"All right," she retorted, fuming, "I'll pack my bags and you can take me to Tucson first thing tomorrow." She wasn't about to tell him that she couldn't afford a fancy resort and that after he dropped her off, she would be forced to call a cab for the airport and hop the next flight home to Milwaukee. But wasn't that what she'd been telling herself she should do anyway?

She watched as he hurled a shovelful of dirt onto the ground behind him. Then she turned on her heel and stalked off.

She was striding past Romeo and Juliet when she felt a warm male hand touch her arm.

"Please . . . wait."

Something in the tone of Reece's voice made her stop. Maybe it was the undertone of contriteness. She glanced up; a look of chagrin clouded his features.

"I apologize. I was way out of line. I—" He raked a hand through his hair and stared past her at the statues. "I want you to stay." His gaze returned to hers. "Will you?" he asked.

Standing that close to him in the shadow of the star-crossed lovers, all Callie could think of was the momentary peace she had found in his arms, and so she said, "I'll think about it."

Chapter Three

Hugging her sides, Callie stared out her window at the sculpture garden. She'd been trying to convince herself that she was a fool for telling Reece that she'd think about staying on at the inn. She'd blown the perfect opportunity when she'd rejected his offer to take her to Tucson—and away from Casa de la Rosa Blanca. Granted, he'd hit a sore spot in accusing her of being uptight. She *was* uptight.

Despite her vow to follow Dr. Simmons's orders and simply relax on her vacation, she felt on edge and driven like some madwoman by a sense of urgency that she couldn't define. She could blame it on old habits, or her pressure-cooker job where deadlines and demands on her time were the order of the day. But if she were honest, she'd be forced to admit that the cause was more rooted in her heart than her head.

Because the weeks, the months have taken on a numbing sameness, she concluded. *Because it's the way I've grown used to coping with the loneliness, the disillusionment.*

She couldn't help but notice that Reece's actions, his words, betrayed impatience too—as if he were in a hurry to get his life over with.

What does he do to pass the hours? she wondered. *Spend his days digging up prickly ocotillos and his nights roaming among the statues in the courtyard, serenading them with love songs?*

When she'd asked him if he liked living in the desert, he'd hesitated before answering that he'd gotten used to it. Had he gradually grown accustomed to the isolation too, so that he preferred his own company to that of others? Yet he *had* asked her to stay, and she knew she hadn't misread the look of pleading in his gaze.

And the truth was, she wanted to stay. But it scared her to acknowledge that her reasons for wanting to stay on had more to do with him than with any burning desire to find and photograph Vulture's Creek.

She pressed her cheek against the windowpane; the sun scalded her cheek through the thin layer of glass, and she drew back. Though she was still full from breakfast, a check of her watch told her that it was half past noon. She thought of skipping lunch, then decided she could manage a salad at least and something cool to drink.

She sat at the same table in the dining room; a crystal vase filled with fresh-cut flowers graced the table.

"Mr. Tanner orders them weekly from a florist in Tucson," Elena said as she set a mixed green salad in front of Callie. "It is a tradition the Bennetts started when they first owned the inn. Like the candles that are lit in the lobby each evening."

Callie unfolded her napkin and placed it in her lap. "They're very lovely traditions," she said sincerely. "And I would say your cooking alone should be enough to attract hordes of tourists."

The housekeeper's face beamed with a gentle smile. "Thank you, Miss Townsend. But I'm afraid the big hotels in the cities have much more to offer than we do here at Casa de la Rosa Blanca. You know, I was born not so far from here, and I have lived for a long while in this area. But things have changed. A quiet way of life has passed in favor of one that—" She suddenly frowned. "Change is not always for the better, Miss Townsend." She fell silent for a moment as she plucked a dead leaf from the bouquet. "I had an older brother," she said quietly. "His name was

Luis. When the Vietnam War came, he decided that he must do something to help the orphaned children in that country. So he went over there to work in a mission home. There was a village near the orphanage. Luis was in the village picking up supplies for the mission when the planes came, carrying bombs. The village, the orphanage . . . everything was destroyed in an instant of time.''

Callie set a forkful of salad down without eating it. ''I'm sorry,'' she said, thinking how trite the words sounded—and how many times over the past year she'd heard them from the lips of well-meaning friends and colleagues.

''War—killing of any sort—is a terrible thing. So many lives ruined, families torn apart, their happiness destroyed. Perhaps that's why I chose not to marry.'' She raised her eyes to the window. ''Perhaps that is the reason others find themselves alone too.''

At first Callie guessed that Elena was thinking of the vagrant who had died at Vulture's Creek. But when she followed Elena's gaze, she knew differently. Her throat constricted at the sight of Reece framed in the window. After a second he went on, and Elena turned back to the table.

''Did you speak to him about Vulture's Creek?'' she asked.

Callie took a swallow of iced tea before answering. ''Yes. As I thought, he's not interested in conducting tours to ghost towns.''

Elena smiled softly. ''I'm sure, Miss Townsend, that with persuasion you will be able to convince him to take you there.''

Callie finished her salad mechanically, without tasting it. She wondered if Elena had knowledge of something in Reece's background that would explain why he chose to live as he did at an out-of-the-way inn rarely frequented by guests. Maybe he'd confided in the housekeeper, though that seemed unlikely to Callie. Or he could have made a casual remark that had hinted at his past and caused Elena to draw certain conclusions. Or maybe Elena, like Ada Hawk, had guessed at his reasons.

She found herself admiring Elena, not only for her graciousness but for her obvious acceptance of her circumstances in life.

Will I ever be able to do the same? Callie asked herself.

She ate very little of the rest of her meal and left the table with a feeling of guilt for not devouring every bite after praising Elena on her culinary abilities.

Wandering into the lobby, she perused the spines of the books on the shelves. *Nothing much of interest here,* she concluded. Most of the volumes looked ancient and bore stodgy-sounding titles like *The History of Roman Civilization.* She was about to give up her search for something to read when a book on the bottom shelf caught her eye.

"*Ghost Towns and Mining Camps of the Southwest,*" Callie read under her breath. She pulled out the volume and set it aside. If Reece wasn't going to take her to Vulture's Creek, then maybe this book would teach her something about the town.

After trading her jeans for a pair of cotton shorts and donning her walking shoes, she slathered sunscreen on her face, arms, and legs. Then she hung her camera around her neck. She placed the strap of her camera case over one shoulder and tucked the book on ghost towns under her arm.

The couples seemed to follow her with their sad eyes as she passed through the sculpture garden. Whipped by a hot breeze, the wiry arms of the ocotillo set up a brittle chattering that caused her to recall Reece's warning and give the plant a wide berth.

Callie discovered a footpath that led into the oasis. A feeling of coolness caressed her skin under the lacy canopy of trees. Above the whispering breeze, she thought she heard the notes of a songbird. She found the spa, a large, square tub encircled by an attractive redwood deck. Walking deeper into the grove, she spied one of the hammocks stretched between the sturdy branches of a towering cottonwood.

She made herself comfortable in the hammock. The mosaic of green leaves and blue heaven above were soothing to the senses, and she laid the book aside for a moment.

After finding the view of trees and sky that most pleased her, she outfitted her camera with a soft-focus filter from the camera case. Then she shot several frames of the overhead scene.

The quiet of the oasis seemed to lull her into a state of drowsiness. Maybe the languid feeling came from knowing that away from the trees, the land lay broiling in the hot stillness of a Sonoran afternoon. Whatever the reason, she closed her eyes and dozed off, thinking that she hadn't forgotten, after all, how to relax and enjoy herself.

Chink. Chink.

Callie woke with a start—and nearly tumbled out of the hammock. Her heartbeat hammered in her ears; her hands clutched at her camera and the book to keep them from tumbling to the ground. She had no recollection of sleeping, but she knew that she'd been dreaming of Nolan.

It was the same horrific nightmare that had jolted her awake countless times in the cold, dark nights following his death. She hadn't had the dream in months, but she could recall every vivid detail of the gruesome vision in which he was frantically trying to claw his way out of the snowbanked ground at Maple Lawn Cemetery.

She held her head in her hands and attempted to shake the ghoulish thought from her mind.

Chink. Chink.

For a moment she believed that she was still dreaming and the sound came from Nolan pounding in desperation against the locked steel lid of his casket. Her hands trembled as she got out of the hammock. Gone was any semblance of peace that she'd briefly entertained. The leafy canopy above seemed to cast a gloomy pall over the ground; the breeze no longer refreshed her.

Chink. Chink.

A nervous laugh escaped her. The noise was real, not a figment of her imagination. It echoed through the trees so that she wasn't certain which direction it came from. Confused, she picked up the book and her camera case and set off on a path that she hoped would lead her to the source of the sound. She passed a spring burbling up from the earth. Water from the spring cascaded merrily over a series of rock ledges, finally spilling into a narrow creekbed lined with pebbles. Just past the spring the oasis ended at the edge of a clearing.

Callie stopped short at the unexpected sight of Reece in the clearing. He stood in front of an imposing block of granite, his hammer raised in his right hand. A chisel, clutched in his left hand, was placed flush against the stone. Beyond him lay another uncut block of stone and, beyond that, a corrugated metal shed that looked to be in an alarming state of disrepair. A long table near the shed held an assortment of tools.

Reece was turned away so that he couldn't see her, though she had a plain view of him from where she stood in the shadow of a clump of bushes.

Chink. Chink. Chink.

Reece brought the hammer down on the chisel time and again, sending tiny shards of stone flying through the air.

When he paused and looked around, Callie saw that he wore a pair of protective glasses to shield his eyes, and she recalled a remark of Ada's that had seemed odd to her. Something to Reece about being blinded by chips from boulders.

Callie thought she knew what Ada was referring to. Reece himself had created the statues in the courtyard.

He dropped the hammer, tore off the glasses, and reached for a canteen that was propped against the block of stone. Callie could hear his thirsty gulps as he downed whatever was in the container. Her pulse raced when he stripped off his shirt and wiped away the perspiration.

Without thought, she let the book on ghost towns fall to the ground as she hurried to change the lens on the camera and adjust the lens aperture and focus.

There. She had him framed perfectly. She snapped a picture. In the silence, the noise of the shutter release sounded like a gunshot in Callie's ears.

Reece pivoted in her direction, and she quickly ducked behind the bushes, berating herself for forgetting to take into account the noisiness of the Nikon. She anticipated what excuse she'd concoct if Reece suddenly pounced on her, demanding to know what she was doing there. Maybe *It isn't a crime to take someone's picture, is it?* Or *I didn't see a No Trespassing sign in the vicinity.*

She peeked over the top of the bushes and saw with relief that Reece was rummaging through the assortment of tools that lay on the table beside the shed.

She tore her gaze from the sight of his back and made herself turn away. She followed the path of the creek, heedless of where she was going. She told herself she wouldn't get completely lost as long as she didn't stray far from the little stream. Her notion that she had found a measure of tranquillity in the oasis had been shattered by her nightmare, and by her discovery that Reece was near, carving lovers out of stone.

Why was he so fascinated by star-crossed lovers? Callie suspected they were a reflection of himself—never revealing more than what was plainly visible on the surface. Or maybe he was driven as an artist to create the unusual, just as she often photographed things that people in general neither cared about nor took note of. Like the leaning, rusted stop sign she'd happened across at the end of a rural Wisconsin lane. Or a red high-heeled shoe she'd found stuck at a garish angle in a bank of snow.

The oasis ended abruptly at a place where the creekbed widened and meandered away into nothingness. Ahead of Callie, an endless track of barren earth led up to the far mountains. The land drowsed in the midst of a yellow haze.

Heat seemed to rise from the desert floor. She sensed that somewhere in that expanse lay Vulture's Creek.

Callie scanned the horizon. A small cloud of dust was visible in the distance. Like a minitornado, it rose and swirled across the ground, growing larger as it made a zig-zag approach in her direction. She started to turn away, then saw the figure of someone on a bicycle in the middle of the cloud. The next thing she knew the bicycle emerged from the dusty veil and careened to a stop precariously near her toes.

A young boy wearing patched jeans and a dirty T-shirt hopped off the bicycle. Callie estimated the youngster to be about ten or eleven.

He let the bicycle fall to the ground. "Hi," he said, peering at her with huge, intelligent brown eyes. "You must be the new guest."

With his engaging grin and mop of shiny black hair, the boy was definitely a charmer. "How did you know?"

He shrugged. "Easy. Pale skin. No hat. Bad shoes."

Callie looked down at her feet. First Reece had criticized her for wearing sandals—though not without some merit, she had to admit. Now this kid acted dubious about her homely Rockports. "Why do you say 'bad shoes'?"

"Cheap leather."

"Cheap leather, my eye!" she retorted. "I paid very good money for this pair of Rockports."

He grinned mischievously. "Doesn't matter. Grandpa Aguilar says a rattler's fangs'll go through shoe leather faster than a bolt of lightning'll split a cottonwood in two."

Callie winced at the vivid metaphor. But the name Aguilar struck a bell. "Your grandfather works at the inn, doesn't he?"

"Yeah. I help him sometimes."

"By the way, my name's Callie Townsend," she said, figuring an introduction was in order. "What's yours?"

"Marcos."

"Do you live close by, Marcos?"

"About a couple of miles down the road."

Callie squinted into the distance but saw no sign of a house, only the ever-present saguaro and scrub brush. "Ada Hawk told me that your grandfather lives at the inn."

"Sometimes, when he has extra work to do. But mostly he lives with us."

"Do you have a big family?"

Marcos shoved his hands in his jeans pockets. "Kind of. My mom and dad and two sisters and a brother."

"Okay, now that I know so much about you, Marcos, what do you recommend I do so that I'm not in danger of a rattler sniping at my toes?"

He grinned. "Get some boots." He yanked up his pant legs to reveal a pair of scuffed but sturdy-looking black boots with spiffy red and blue trim. "Mom bought mine at Buckskin Bill's in Tucson."

"Hmm. I've never heard of Buckskin Bill's."

Marcos stared soberly at her feet. "One of my sisters has feet only a little larger than yours. She could loan you a pair of boots. She's got at least three."

Callie suppressed a smile. "I appreciate that, but I couldn't. . . . I'll tell you what, Marcos. I'll see if I can buy a pair somewhere. If not, then maybe I'll take you up on your offer. All right?"

"All right." He bowed his head and kicked a stone out of the way of the bicycle's front tire. "I better get going. I'm supposed to help Grandpa paint the fence at the inn."

What fence? Callie wondered. Suddenly she had an idea. "Before you go, could you tell me where Vulture's Creek is? No one else seems to know how to get there."

He curved his brown fingers around the handlebars of the bike. "Mr. Tanner knows where it is."

I'll bet, thought Callie.

Marcos grinned. "But I can *show* you. You want me to take you there tomorrow?"

"Yes . . . sure. But aren't you in school?"

"Nah. The teachers have in-service days this week.

They're all in Nogales." He frowned. "But maybe you'd better get the boots first."

"Then how about day after tomorrow?"

"Okay. I'll meet you here," he said. "One o'clock," he called over his shoulder as he rode off.

"It's a date," Callie whispered. But where was she going to find a place that sold boots before day after tomorrow? And how much of her mad money would she have to blow on a pair?

It wasn't until later, when night was closing in, that Callie realized she'd left the book on ghost towns back at the edge of the clearing. She'd gone up to her room after eating her evening meal alone. Her intention had been to outfit her camera with a different lens so that she could snap some photos of the statues by moonlight.

She wondered if she should attempt to search for the book instead. What if it rained before dawn? The book would be ruined—and she'd have to explain her carelessness to Reece. On the other hand, any chance of rain appeared slim, considering there wasn't a cloud to be seen in the sky. The view out her window looked dark and foreboding, except for a full moon the size and color of a ripe cantaloupe peeking over the roof of the inn. She decided she'd take her chances with the weather and wait for morning to retrieve the book.

She got her collapsible tripod from the closet where Elena had stored it, and loaded her camera with a fresh roll of film. Soft music and softer candlelight greeted her in the lobby. Her gaze swept the shadowy corners of the room, and she tried to envision a time when the lobby teemed with guests and lively conversation.

She circled the room and took pictures of the impressive fireplace and of the painting of the white rose. Then she went outside and set up her tripod near the statues of Romeo and Juliet. The yard was quiet; there was no guitar serenade that evening. She glanced toward the row of windows under the porch. A single light burned in one of them. She saw a curtain move. Then the light went out, and all the windows wore dark, blank faces.

For a while she lost herself in her work. By the time she finished the last of the roll of film, the air had taken on a decided nip. She folded her tripod and tucked it under her arm. Her hand brushed against something warm—another hand.

She drew in a sharp breath and turned. The hand was Balzac's. The stone fingers had apparently retained the heat they'd absorbed from the sun.

Staring at the beautifully chiseled body, she thought of Reece as she'd seen him that afternoon, his lean, powerful body gilded by the sun. She remembered the comfort of being clasped against him under the cool light of the moon. It had been so long since she'd known the comfort of an intimate embrace, the joy of being told she was beautiful and loved. For one wild moment she yearned for such happiness again.

I mustn't think of it now, she admonished herself. *The setting, the man, the timing—it's all wrong. What I need in my life right now is a sense of security and stability, not a romance with some mystery man who lives in the desert and spends his days chiseling couples out of stone.*

She fairly ran the length of the garden to the inn. Closing the door behind her, she shut out the view of the statues and the night.

She went directly up to her room. Vaguely, she noted that a new fat white candle replaced the one from the night before in the wall sconce. She let down her hair in front of the mirror and brushed it until it shone. She started to put on her cotton gown.

Before she went to bed, she took her journal from the bureau and a pen from her purse. The journal fell open to an entry. It was dated September 12.

Dashed out to the mall for some last-minute purchases. I handled the crowds well. No anxiety! Am beginning to feel more positive about my trip to Arizona.

The entry seemed an eternity ago to Callie. She turned the page to record her impressions of the Sonoran Desert and Case de la Rosa Blanca. Instead, the words that flowed from her pen were about couples meeting secretly in the dark, caught up in a web of futile dreams.

Chapter Four

" "I see you've decided to stay."

Callie raised her head at the sound of Reece's voice. She found him standing by the table where she'd been eating her breakfast. "For now," she conceded. Her eyes were drawn to the book he held in his hands.

"I believe you left this behind yesterday," he said, handing her the volume on ghost towns.

"I—" Had he known then that she'd been watching him the day before?

He let the book fall onto the table by her plate. "The book's yours to keep if you want it."

"It is?"

"Yep."

Callie returned his smile. "Thank you."

"No problem." He leaned closer. "I'm heading to town to the market, if you'd care to go along. You might be interested to know that Ada carries a decent assortment of straw hats—whatever suits your style."

"Why not?" she said. His invitation sounded far more appealing than the idea of lying in a hammock all afternoon. "Does Ada carry leather boots too?"

"No, but there's a place in town that does."

"Town? I thought Hawk's Market was . . . it."

"You thought wrong." Reece made room for her as she

43

got up from the table. The touch of his hand stopped her. "Why're you interested in boots?"

"Because a rattler's fangs'll go through shoe leather faster than a bolt of lightning'll split a cottonwood."

"Where'd you hear that?"

"Isn't it just common sense?" she responded, not about to clue him in on the fact that she'd met a young boy who'd shown more willingness than he had to lead her Vulture's Creek.

Reece regarded her curiously. "I'm leaving in half an hour," he said.

The first thing Callie noticed when she climbed into the vehicle was that Reece had been true to his word concerning the air conditioner. The interior of the van was pleasantly cool—a good thing, since the day was already stiflingly hot.

"Might as well sit up front," he said as she headed for the bench seat. "The view's better."

So she sat with him in front. Peering out the window, she saw that there wasn't a cloud in sight in the swath of sapphire sky stretching to the horizon.

"It'll rain later," Reece predicted.

"It doesn't look like rain," she said.

"Trust me."

The words sounded in Callie's head and she slumped in her seat, lost for a moment in a snare of bitter memories.

"Trust me." It was one of the last things Nolan had told her before his death. She'd been perturbed over the late hours he'd been keeping at the bank where he was employed as chief loan officer. He had attempted to still her concerns with a string of reassurances and a lingering kiss.

When she'd protested, he'd held her tighter, vowing that soon, very soon, he'd cut back on his schedule, that he would make it up to her with a honeymoon she'd never forget. *"Acapulco, Monaco, St. Croix, Aruba. Whatever your heart desires, babe,"* he'd whispered in her ear. She'd started to tell him that she'd rather head north to Lake Superior and rent a cabin on one of the Apostle Islands, but he'd hushed her with the fatal words: *"Trust me."* Too late she'd realized how tragically flawed her vision of Nolan Jamison had been.

The crackle of the radio intruded on her thoughts. For once she was grateful that she could sit and stare out the dusty window of the van and listen to the strains of a sad country song instead of having to invent something to say.

Callie began to notice that the Sonoran wasn't as barren as she'd first imagined. The stately saguaro still dominated the landscape, though here and there stands of the odd-looking ocotillo plants dotted the ground. But outnumbering every other type of vegetation was a sea of what appeared to be stunted evergreens. And there was even an occasional lone cottonwood, its trunk bent like the back of a very old man, its limbs twisted and half stripped of leaves from a losing battle with the elements.

The area was not as flat as she'd believed, either. In the distance a series of undulating ochre hills, each a little higher and lighter than the one before it, marched all the way to the mountains until it was impossible to discern where the hills left off and the mountains began.

The music on the radio came to an abrupt halt.

"Those mountains aren't as treeless as you might think," Reece offered.

Glancing at him, she found his dark eyes observing her for a second.

"Go thirty or so miles into the mountains," he said, giving his attention to the road again, "and you'll find a subalpine forest. Firs. Pine trees. Lakes and trails. Wildflowers. We pasture our horses in one of the meadows over the summer. We'll be bringing them down now in a couple more weeks."

"You have horses? I didn't see any stable."

"We have a corral and a small barn. There are two roan geldings and a chestnut mare. Used to be six, but the Ben-

netts had me sell off three to a dude ranch in New Mexico.'' He paused. ''Do you ride?''

''Me? Ah . . .'' She'd never been on a horse in her life.

''I'll take that as a no,'' he said, and switched the radio
back on.

While yet another song played out a familiar tale of un-
requited love, Callie stared at the mountains and tried to
visualize forests of green fir and pine trees clinging to their
steep sides, and a meadow where two roan geldings and a
chestnut mare had nothing more to concern themselves with
than to romp through the wildflowers and bask in the sunshine. She found herself envying them, and she wondered
if Reece visited the horses often. She hadn't asked him if
he knew how to ride, but she assumed that he did. She
envisioned him astride one of the geldings, his hair slicked
back by the wind, his profile exuding a quiet power and
strength as he urged the horse on, like something out of an
old romantic Western. But was he the hero or the villain
in her make-believe story?

Finally, Hawk's Market came into view, a dot in the
distance, and Callie suddenly realized that she'd forgotten
her camera. When she'd taken the book on ghost towns up
to her room for safekeeping, she'd meant to pick up her
camera and a fresh roll of film. Instead, the half hour Reece
had given her had slipped away while she plaited her hair
in a braid and changed into a fresh pair of jeans and a pale
peach cotton top. Now she regretted her oversight.

A few minutes later, Reece pulled into the parking lot
of the market. There wasn't another vehicle in sight, nor
any sign of Ada's dog. Callie wondered if the market was
closed again. But the *Open* sign glowed brightly in the
window and, to Callie's surprise, Ada stood waiting at the
door for her two customers to pile out of the van.

''It's about time ya got here,'' she said gruffly in greeting to Reece. ''You, too, missy,'' she added with a curt
nod in Callie's direction.

Callie went ahead of Reece into the store. Several ceiling

fans buzzed noisily overhead where rows of bare lightbulbs hung above the aisles of goods for sale. She hadn't noticed the fans and naked bulbs during her first foray into the market. But then finding a drink to ease the tickle in her throat had been a priority.

"Miss Townsend's looking for a hat," Reece said from behind Callie.

Ada eyed Callie from head to foot. " 'S that so? Well, I hope you ain't too particular, missy." Turning to Reece, she said, "Doc an' I been chewin' the fat long enough, waitin' for ya to get here."

Callie followed the sweep of Ada's gnarly hand to where a stooped, white-haired man sat on a chair by the counter. A cane rested on the back of the chair.

"His supplies are boxed up an' ready to go," Ada went on. "Got a fresh-cooked chicken dinner out of me with his sweet talkin', too. Spoiled plenty, he is, I'd say."

Reece chuckled. "I wouldn't worry, Ada. I have a feeling you'd miss spoiling him if he weren't around."

Ada sniffed and shot a glance at Callie. "Come on over, missy, and meet Doc."

At their approach, the older man slowly got up from the chair. He wobbled unsteadily, and Reece stepped in, lending him a hand.

Callie observed the gentle care with which Reece helped the frail man gain his footing, and she remembered the way his strong arms had reached out to steady her that night in the courtyard. She saw too that Doc's left arm and hand hung uselessly at his side, and the corner of his mouth drooped down.

"Doc, this here pretty young lady's one of the guests out at the inn," Ada said by way of introduction.

Intelligent blue eyes met Callie's. "Evan Stoner," the older man said with a slight thickness to his words. "And what might this pretty young lady's name be?"

"Callie," she said. "Callie Townsend."

The blue eyes sparkled. "The pleasure's all mine, Callie," Evan Stoner said with a slight bow.

Over Doc's head, Reece grinned at her. "I'll be gone about an hour. I'm sure Ada will be happy to entertain you until I get back."

Callie watched as Reece guided Evan Stoner around the counter. The older man turned and dipped another little bow in her direction before he went out the door. She smiled and raised her hand in a wave.

"Here ya are, missy," Ada called out from down one of the aisles.

Callie found Ada near the back of the store, standing in front of a shelf heaped with hats.

Ada grinned. "Maybe there'll be one that'll tickle your fancy. Mirror's to your right by the soda cooler. When you're ready to buy, I'll be at the counter."

Callie eyed the piles of hats with some trepidation. Ignoring the Stetsons that were stacked together, she randomly pulled out several of the straw hats. After considerable debate, she decided on a broad-brimmed number decorated with imitation silver and turquoise studs, reasoning that if she was going to buy Western-style boots, she might as well go all the way with the fake cowgirl image.

"Ya made a decent choice, missy," Ada declared as she handed Callie change for a ten. "Now come with me. I've got something to show ya that you're gonna like."

Callie tagged along with Ada. The older woman opened a door at the rear of the market and motioned for Callie to step through.

The cool, dimly lit room was furnished with a sofa and a chair that were covered with worn blue chenille throws. Magazines and books spilled over the sides of a coffee table that looked like it had been plucked from a Dumpster.

Ada switched on a floor lamp, illuminating an upright piano with a vase of plastic flowers gracing the top. A china cabinet stood in elegant contrast to the painfully shabby furnishings. Opposite the piano, an archway revealed a view of a stove and a dinette set with two chairs.

"Why don't ya take a seat," Ada invited.

Callie sat in the chair. The cushion sagged beneath her. Too late she realized that Chico was asleep beside the chair. She eyed the mongrel skeptically.

"Don't worry, missy. Chico won't hurt ya. He loves company. Don't ya, boy?" Ada added softly.

The dog raised his head and cocked an ear in his mistress's direction. His tail thumped twice; then his head dropped down again, and his eyes shut in peaceful repose.

It was miraculous, Callie considered. The animal lying quietly beside her bore no similarity to the vicious beast that Reece had calmed only nights before.

"Do ya play the piano, missy?"

Callie gave her attention to Ada. "I never have. Do you, Ada?" Was this to be the entertainment that Reece had hinted at?

"Nope. My husband, Clifford, did." Ada ambled over to the piano. "He sang too. Sweetest music I ever heard was when he serenaded me with songs on this here instrument." She ran her hand over the closed keyboard. "Hauled this piano all the way out from Missouri, where we was from. Hard to believe it was more than forty years ago."

"Was it difficult for you . . . that is, leaving Missouri and coming to the desert?"

Ada chuckled. "Thinkin' back, I'd say that nothin' seems too difficult when you're young an' in love." She set keen eyes on Callie. "You ever been in love, missy?"

"I . . ." Callie's throat constricted. She looked away for a moment.

"Had your heart broken, have ya? I reckon the same's wrong with Reece Tanner. Somethin' terrible happened to him, I tell ya. I been around long enough to know the signs." She turned to the china cabinet. "Reece's got goodness in him underneath all that guff he dishes out." The glass door on the cabinet squeaked when she pulled it open on its hinges. "Bet your bottom dollar he's easy as mush inside, just like Clifford was. Lookit the way he lends a helpin' hand to folks like Doc Stoner."

Ada shook her head. "Doc delivered nearly all the babies in these parts. Knew his medicine right well too. Came by to see my Clifford every day toward the last. Accepted his pay in canned goods and vegetables. Then Doc himself took ill with a stroke. Still a charmer, though, ain't he?" She laughed. "Now, missy, this is what I wanted to show ya. My pots."

She removed a teapot from one of the shelves. "Here's my Lindsay pattern. Belonged to my mother."

Callie admired the cheerful hand-painted floral design, the pretty yellow china rosebud perched on the lid. "It's lovely."

"Made in a village way off in Hungary. Got the creamer and sugar bowl to match." Ada took them down from the shelf for Callie to see, then put them back. "Now this is Bavarian," she said, pointing to a white teapot splashed with delicate violets. "Clifford bought it for me on our twentieth weddin' anniversary. See, there's a whole breakfast set." She pointed with a knobby finger to a pair of matching cups and saucers and a creamer and sugar bowl.

"But this last one's my favorite. Called a chocolate pot." She offered it to Callie for inspection. "Got the surprise of my life when Reece came in one day, totin' a package all wrapped up with a yellow bow. Told me it was a gift for me. Said, 'Go on ahead and open it, Ada.' An' I did, and this here chocolate pot was inside. Said he'd found it in some little shop in Phoenix."

Callie fingered the tall, graceful-looking pot with its design of delicate pale pink roses and green leaves. "It's absolutely beautiful," she said, trying to picture Reece scouting out teapots in a little shop in Phoenix.

"Glad ya like it. Too bad Reece's come for ya already or I'd make ya a cup of hot chocolate in it."

Callie looked past Ada to where Reece stood in the doorway. His eyes locked with hers for a moment as Ada took the pot from her hands.

"Go on with ya then, missy," Ada said, shooing her off. "I don't have time to sit around with ya all day."

Callie felt the barest brush of Reece's fingers on her wrist as she moved past him. A streak of warmth shot up her arm from where he had touched her skin. She told herself the contact was purely accidental on his part. Then his hand came to rest for a second on her elbow, and when she looked up, she saw a teasing glint in his eyes.

"Didn't I tell you you'd be entertained?" he said.

Before they left the market, Reece had a private word with Ada while Callie stood in front of the mirror, fixing her new hat on her head.

"Sensible hat," Reece remarked as they crossed the parking lot to the van. "Attractive too," he added.

"Thanks," Callie said, smiling.

"You're welcome," he replied.

They rode a short distance down the highway; then Reece turned the van onto a side road. They passed a tiny graveyard enclosed by a high iron fence. In the distance a clump of trees loomed in a blue-gray haze above the flat surroundings. Callie guessed correctly that they were approaching Rio Puerco. She was coming to equate the presence of trees in the desert with civilization.

As they neared the village, the low shapes of buildings came into view, sturdy, one-story structures built of adobe.

Reece pulled the van into a parking space in front of a plaza that was bordered on three sides by the buildings. In the center of the plaza, shaded by a leafy bower of cottonwood trees, stood a tiny gazebo painted white with yellow trim. Several elderly men sat on the benches that lined the walk leading up to the gazebo. Two other men, wearing Stetsons and smoking cigars, sat opposite each other at a picnic table, playing a game of cards.

"What do you think of Rio Puerco now?" Reece asked.

"It's charming," Callie said, captivated by the sight of the quaint-looking shops with colorful signs hanging from hooks above their doors or in their curtained windows.

"There's a café across the way that serves some great Mexican food." He gestured in the direction of a building that sported a line of wind socks tied to its red-tiled roof. "That is, if you're hungry for lunch." He cast a sideways glance at her. "Or you could shop for boots first."

"Lunch sounds good." She could hardly believe she was so hungry when she'd eaten breakfast only a couple of hours ago. Maybe it was the clear, dry desert air that had suddenly sparked her appetite. Or, she acknowledged a little reluctantly, maybe it was the company she was keeping.

Reece ushered her toward the restaurant. *Cantina de la Garcia* the sign in the window announced.

A lively tune sung in Spanish played from an old-fashioned jukebox that pulsed with a rainbow of neon-colored lights. Animated conversation in the same tongue rose over the music from the olive-skinned men and women seated around several tables scattered about the room. Delightful, spicy smells permeated the air.

Heads turned as Callie followed Reece to a table in the rear, and she felt the other patrons' eyes tracking her. Curiosity about the stranger in town, she supposed.

Reece pulled out a chair for her. She took off her hat and brushed back a stray wisp of hair from her forehead.

"This isn't the quietest place in the world," Reece said, his face dipped low to hers.

The hot rush of his breath on her cheek caught Callie by surprise. His hand hovered on the arm of her chair, inches from hers. She noted the sprinkling of silky black hairs on the back of his hand, the long, tapered fingers. There were calluses on his thumb and forefinger, and she thought of him with a hammer raised in his right hand, ready to strike chisel to stone.

"Well, would you look at what the bobcat drug in."

Callie's head jerked up at the sound of the low, sultry

voice. Her gaze moved past Reece to the woman approaching the table.

"Hello, Darla."

"Aw, Reece, honey, now what kind of greeting is that?" The woman he'd called Darla sidled up to him. She placed her hands on her hips and raked her gaze over Reece. Her flame red curls framed a face painted flawlessly with makeup. Tight pants and a satiny lilac top clung to every curve of the woman's body.

Reece made no response as he brushed by her and seated himself in the chair opposite Callie.

Darla plopped an open menu in front of him. She tossed another one, closed, in Callie's direction along with a measuring glance. "Special today's your favorite," she said, cozying up to Reece again. "Blue corn enchiladas," she purred, "and sides of Ray's special beans and chorizo."

"Sounds good," Reece said. "Ice water to drink. And a cup of coffee—black." He looked over his menu at Callie. "The lady'll need a few minutes to decide. She's a guest at the inn, wanted to come to town to do a little shopping."

Darla swiveled in Callie's direction. "Staying long?" she asked in a saccharine tone.

Callie lifted her chin and smiled. "A month. And I don't need time to study the menu. If Reece is having the special, then I will too, except iced tea to drink." Too late she realized his name had slipped off her tongue in a strangely familiar way.

Darla's crimson mouth screwed into a scowl as she scribbled down the order. She started off, then stopped and leaned close to Reece. "You haven't forgotten about the dance Saturday at the club, have you, sweetheart?"

The smile froze on Callie's face as a ridiculous jolt of envy knifed through her at the idea of Reece escorting the voluptuous Darla to a dance.

"Haven't forgotten," he said, "but I can't promise I'll be there." His gaze shifted for an instant toward Callie, and there was a hint of humor in his eyes. "Not with so much to look after at the inn."

"I'm sure your guests can spare your services for one night," Darla retorted. She leveled a frigid glance at Callie, then sauntered away.

"I take it you're in great demand around town whenever there's a dance," Callie said, thinking that perhaps Reece wasn't as much of a loner as she'd imagined.

Reece gave a dry chuckle and studied his folded hands. "Folks around here hold more dances than a horsefly has eyes. It's all for a noble cause, though. The money they raise goes to buy goods to stock the community's food pantry. There's a lot of unemployment in the region. Jobs that are available pay low wages. Some people wouldn't be able to put dinner on the table for their families if it weren't for the food pantry."

"People like Doc Stoner."

Reece looked up. "Doc pays for his own groceries."

"But you and Ada pad his order so that he has enough to eat." A muscle twitched in Reece's jaw, alerting Callie that she'd hit on the truth. "Ada said you're very good to Doc."

"I'm not doing anything for Doc that he hasn't already done for others."

Callie remembered Ada's revealing comment that the doctor had taken his pay from her in canned goods during her husband's illness. Ada had said too that Reece was soft as mush inside. Thanks to the older woman, she'd learned a few things about Reece that day, and she liked what she'd heard.

Darla returned with the water and iced tea. She plunked the tea in front of Callie and set the water by Reece's hand. "Food's coming," she announced.

Callie tore open a packet of sugar and stirred it in her tea. "I have a feeling the waitress is upset that you didn't give her a definite answer about the dance."

Reece took a slow sip from his glass. "Darla's not exactly a waitress. She owns the café."

"Oh . . ." Callie felt herself blushing.

"I don't care to attend the dances in town," he said, observing her over the rim of his glass. "I prefer to do my dancing under the moon and stars, not in some crowded, smoky nightclub."

An image of him dancing under the moon and stars flooded Callie's head. Dancing with her, that was, holding her close while he hummed the "Sonoran Love Song" in her ear.

Careful, a voice inside her head warned. Yet how could she ever hope to fully heal, to let go of the past, if she didn't begin to trust her instincts again, to believe in the possibility that she could meet a man who had a good heart and honorable intentions—even if he seemed reluctant to open up and talk about himself?

He looked at her as if he knew she'd been imagining herself in his arms. "I think you're going to be in for a shock when you taste your enchiladas."

Callie blinked and saw that their food had arrived. She caught a glimpse of Darla's curvy hips as the woman strutted off. "What do you mean?" she asked Reece.

"The blue corn enchiladas are hotter than a fiery desert sunset," Reece said. "I'd guess your palate's not used to food this spicy."

"I can handle it," Callie dished back, not about to confess that *spicy* to her meant Chicago-style pizza with extra pepperoni topping.

"You sure? The chorizo—Mexican sausage—is no tame dish either."

"Watch me." She promptly cut off a large forkful of the enchilada and brought it to her mouth. She chewed and swallowed the bite. "See, I'm fine," she said. The words were barely out when a blaze ignited in her mouth. Her ears burned. Tears streamed from her eyes, and she felt like the fire-breathing dragon in a kid's fairy tale.

"Ah . . ." she croaked. She reached for her iced tea, draining the glass in unladylike gulps in an attempt to douse the heat searing her throat and tongue. "I never—"

"Tasted anything that hot?" Reece finished for her.

She looked at him through bleary eyes. He was grinning from ear to ear. Then he started to laugh. Her temper flared. How dared he make fun when she had almost choked to death! Then all of a sudden she found herself laughing along with him. More tears cascaded down her face as a fresh wave of laughter assaulted her.

Reece handed her a napkin, which for some reason set them both off again. Callie swiped at her tears with the napkin. It was totally ridiculous—the two of them sitting there, uproarious.

Suddenly she didn't care that others around them were staring, that Darla was shooting a venomous glance her way from across the room. She didn't care whether she could trust her instincts about Reece Tanner or not. All she knew at that moment was that she was having fun. She was laughing freely, something she realized she hadn't done in in a long time. And it felt good. So good.

Chapter Five

"The locals call it 'walking rain.'"

Callie stared at the horizon where long, delicate streamers trailed from the silver-gray clouds like veils of purple gossamer. "What does that mean—'walking rain'?" she asked Reece, who stood beside her.

"It's from a Native American expression. The rain's falling but it evaporates before it reaches the ground. At the same time, it's on the move as the clouds are driven by the wind."

"Yes . . . I see," she said. "It's beautiful." She'd never have believed that she'd pronounce anything in the desert *beautiful.*

On the way back from Rio Puerco, Reece had turned from the highway onto a rutted gravel road. After driving a couple of miles, he'd pulled onto the shoulder and told Callie there was something he wanted to show her. Then he'd pointed to the clouds on the horizon.

Peeking up at him from under the brim of her hat, Callie decided that, in profile, Reece Tanner looked as hard and unforgiving as the desert itself. But the unexpected tenderness that lit his gaze made her think of Ada's declaration about him. *"Easy as mush inside,"* the older woman had said. Which one was the real Reece Tanner? Callie wished she knew.

"We're going to get a real soaker," Reece said when the rain clouds had moved off to the north.

"How can you tell? The sun's shining again."

He cast her a sideways glance. "After you've lived here awhile, you just know. You can smell the rain, taste it almost."

Callie whiffed the air but detected nothing except the odor of dust.

"Here's another pretty thing." Reece indicated a plant that grew in the dirt a few yards from the shoulder of the road. "Pretty but deadly," he added.

Callie inched closer for a better view. The trunk's thick branches supported clusters of fleshy green stems covered with long, barbed spines.

"I wouldn't go any nearer the jumping cholla if I were you," Reece warned.

Callie did a swift two-step in reverse. "How," she asked, "does the cholla jump?"

Reece chuckled. "Brush against it and the spines'll latch onto your clothes. The segments snap right off, leaving your skin an easy target after the spines work their way through the fabric. Doesn't matter how many layers you're wearing. Worse yet, the needles carry a toxin that causes festering wounds. The cholla's poison's been known to cripple a horse. At night, the cholla's one of the nicest sights around. The moon turns the spines a silvery blond, and the cholla resembles a gorgeous Hollywood starlet out for a stroll. Or maybe you," he said with alarming softness, "with moonbeams playing in your hair, reflecting the color of your eyes."

Warmth flooded Callie's cheeks, and her heart gave a lurch. She had no trouble recalling the way his hair had gleamed like black satin as he walked through his sculpture garden at night. "Is everything in the Sonoran as diabolical as it is pretty?"

His jaw hardened and he looked toward the mountains. "Most everything.

"You know," he said on the way back to the van, "you'll have to break in those boots."

Callie looked from the scuffed toes of his black boots to the shiny toes of her new tan Tony Lama boots. "My boots feel fine," she said a shade stubbornly.

Reece didn't comment, only slid another glance at her as she got into the van.

In fact, Callie was proud of her purchase. The boots fit her like a pair of roomy gloves. When they'd finished their lunch, Reece had directed her to a shop on the square called Boot 'n' Track, where he'd left her to her own devices while he went off on a couple of errands. She'd found the pair of boots with the smart chocolate brown stitching on a sales rack after an eager clerk had tried to steer her in the direction of a high-priced pair. If her boots needed any kind of breaking in, they would get their chance the next day when she wore them on her trek to Vulture's Creek.

The radio sputtered to life as soon as Reece turned the key in the ignition, and Callie settled in the front passenger seat, accustomed by now to the parade of mournful country songs about finding love in all the wrong places.

Two hours later, Callie stood in front of the closet in her room, pondering over what to wear for the evening. For some absurd reason she felt like dressing for dinner, even though she would be eating alone.

When Reece had let her out at the front door of the inn, she'd turned to thank him and stumbled on her words. She'd been almost afraid to lift her gaze to his, fearful he might see that her gratitude extended beyond a few mere words. She'd enjoyed herself in his company—perhaps too much—and for a short time she'd had no thought of panic attacks or that there'd been a cad named Nolan Jamison in her life.

She told herself she would be wise to leave it at that, not to think beyond the fact that Reece had made her laugh and helped her to see that the desert possessed a special majesty of its own. She would have the memory of this day, and—if she were truthful with herself—of the moment when he had caught her in his arms, to fall back on whenever dark images from the past threatened to close in on her again.

But the notion that she'd like to know more, much more, about Reece Tanner teased at her mind. She tried to dismiss the idea as she sorted through the several dresses and ensembles that hung in her closet. She finally settled on an off-the-shoulder white cotton gauze dress with a low, scalloped neckline and a flowing ankle-length skirt. She added a necklace with a pear-shaped amethyst and matching earrings. Before she went downstairs, she spritzed her favorite Vanilla Orchid perfume on the pulse points of her wrists and neck.

"Don't you look lovely tonight!" Elena exclaimed as Callie seated herself at her usual table.

"Thank you," she said with a smile. *All dressed up and no place to go,* she lamented to herself.

Elena crossed her hands over her apron. "Tomorrow evening you'll have company for dinner. Two guests are due in from Chicago in the afternoon."

Callie relished her meal that night—perfectly cooked filet mignon with a grilled vegetable accompaniment. She pondered over what kind of guests she'd be sharing her next dinner with. Hopefully they would be congenial—and show a penchant for exploring ghost towns.

She dawdled over her dessert of fresh fruit and tiny wedges of Camembert. Every now and then her gaze went to the window and the view of Romeo and Juliet with night drawing in around them. She rationalized that she wasn't watching for Reece to appear in the pane of glass. But she found herself questioning where he ate his meals, whether he, too, had dined on filet mignon, and what his plans were for the evening.

When Elena didn't show up to offer her a second cup of coffee, Callie stood and wandered into the lobby.

There was the usual candlelight and classical music and mysterious corners that dissolved into darkness. But something was missing. Callie puzzled over what it was as her eyes took in the bookshelves, the hearth still full of ashes, the paintings of the desert landscapes and of the white—

The white rose. Her gaze returned to the spot where the painting had hung. There was only an outline of dust where the frame had covered the wall.

Callie was disturbed over the picture's disappearance. Maybe it was because the white rose was striking in its simplicity. Or because in her mind it had come to represent the legend connected with the inn.

Finally she left the lobby and flung open the doors to the garden. Moonlight embraced her as she crossed the courtyard. She looked up and saw a ring around the moon, and behind the moon, pewter-lined clouds. There wasn't as much as a hint of a breeze.

This might be the Sonoran Desert instead of Wisconsin, but Callie knew the signs of an impending storm when she saw them. There would be rain, as Reece had predicted.

She heard music drifting through the stillness as she stole among the forest of stately saguaros. She recognized the melody as the "Sonoran Love Song."

At the edge of the trees she hesitated and peered into the yawning depths of the oasis.

"A pretty tune, isn't it?"

Callie turned. Reece was standing just yards away. Her eyes drank in the sight of him as he came toward her. He wore a white shirt and a brown suede vest, his broad shoulders outlined by the play of moonlight behind him. His hair framed his head like a tousled black crown.

"Legend has it that he plays every night when the moon comes over the mountains," Reece went on.

"I thought you were the one who played the guitar."

He laughed. "Me? No. It's the *campesino*."

They stood no more than a foot apart. The scent of musk began to muddle her senses. "Ada told me about the *campesino,* that he was in love with the daughter of the owner of the inn. And that there was a feud."

"Did she say how the story ended?"

"No. She said she didn't believe in such tales."

Reece came another step closer. "Then I'll tell you. Her name was Laurel, her father's, Logan. Logan Mallory. No one seems to recall the name of the *campesino*. The lovers were set to run off together to Mexico. Logan Mallory found out and went gunning for the peasant boy. There'd been a storm. Night was coming fast. Mallory saw movement in the brush where the peasant lay in hiding, waiting for Laurel. Mallory raised his rifle, cocked it, and—"

The music surged, rose to a fever pitch as if the soloist were listening and reliving the story all over again in his mind. Then the tune stopped in midnote. An eerie silence followed.

"And," Callie coaxed.

Reece tilted his head back. His eyes seemed to reflect the moon. Gazing up, Callie realized that Elena was right about the stars in the Sonoran. She'd never seen so many in her life. They twinkled across the night sky like diamonds on a blackened pond. As she watched, one suddenly shot in a flaming streak toward the earth.

"Mallory fixed the *campesino* in the crosshairs," Reece continued. "He fired the rifle once, twice. Then the moon came out from behind a cloud. And Mallory saw that he'd been wrong. It wasn't the peasant boy."

Callie gasped. All the stars seemed to flicker and die. "You mean it was Laurel? Mallory killed his own daughter!"

"That's right," Reece said. The moon was gone from his eyes.

"How do you know all this?"

He shrugged. "It came with the territory. Around here, tales are passed from one generation to the next. The Ben-

netts said they'd found an old diary in one of the rooms.''
He looked at her. ''It was the room that you're staying in.
The whole account was verified in the diary. Later the diary
came up missing. They figured one of the guests had seen
it and decided to take it home as a souvenir.''

''Then the *campesino* is still alive?''

''You don't think a ghost is playing that guitar, do you?''

Callie smiled and shook her head. ''Do you know who
he is?''

Reece's expression grew guarded. ''If I did, I wouldn't
tell. A man's entitled to his privacy, to mourn the way he
chooses—for as long as he needs to.''

A woman too, thought Callie with a cold stab of sorrow.
''How does the white rose figure into the story?''

''The day Mallory buried his daughter, he planted a rosebush in her memory at the grave site. Rumor has it that
one white rose blooms on the bush every year on the anniversary of her death.''

''Have you ever seen the grave . . . and the rosebush?''

''No. My philosophy is that it's best not to go searching
for something that's none of my business.''

''Aren't you a little curious?''

''Not particularly.''

''But is that why you carve statues of couples—as a
tribute to the *campesino* and Laurel?''

Reece looked at the sky. ''When I came here, the courtyard was an overgrown mess. Henry Bennett told me that
I was free to clear out the weeds and do whatever I wanted
with the yard. So I chose to put in a sculpture garden.
Listen,'' he said more softly, ''the peasant's playing the
'Love Song' again. Do you remember what I told you in
the café about dancing?''

Callie felt as if she were falling when Reece brushed a
strand of hair away from her cheek. ''That you liked to do
your dancing under the stars.''

''What about you, Callie?''

This was what she'd dreamed about—Reece taking her

in his arms for a dance that was theirs alone. She deluded herself for a moment into believing she was living that dream, and so she let him guide her hand to rest on his shoulder, allowed herself to smile up at him as he put his hand lightly at her waist and began to lead her through the steps of the waltz.

They moved in harmony, as if in another lifetime they'd been preparing for this moment, this waltz. They swept over the ground in ever-widening circles among the saguaros, in and out of the towering cottonwoods to the strains of the "Sonoran Love Song."

Once, Reece threw back his head and laughed, and it was like the smooth, rushing sound of a stream bubbling over stones. Callie joined in, breathless, half-delirious with the notion that she could go on dancing in his arms under the starry desert sky forever.

Then Reece pulled her closer, and her pulse pounded in her throat. He placed her hand against his vest, and she grasped the buttery fabric in her fingers. His breath stirred her hair as a breeze fluttered through the trees, and the dream gave way to vivid reality.

She sought to memorize his face, to capture his features like a snapshot in her mind so that she could recall them at some point in the future and remember that for a few stolen moments she had known utter happiness.

The "Sonoran Love Song" came to an end. Reece slowed their steps until they stood, motionless, facing each other under the awning of cottonwoods.

He lifted her hair with his hand and let the strands slide through his fingers. She thought of the sculptures in the courtyard and the people they represented—men and women who had loved, laughed, wept, died. "Do you believe in destiny?" she said.

His lips skimmed her brow, her cheek. "I believe in living in the present. It's all we have, Callie. Not the past, not the future. Just now."

She longed for him to say more. He buried his hands in her hair and his mouth covered hers in a long kiss.

When the kiss ended, he said, ''I've wanted to do that since the first time I set eyes on you.'' Slowly, he released her and turned away.

Callie watched, shivering, as he disappeared among the trees like a sleek panther in a forest. She leaned against the cottonwood and closed her eyes. She couldn't think. His kiss had wakened in her a deluge of responses she didn't want to acknowledge, dared not acknowledge. She had come to the Sonoran seeking peace. For a moment, on her first night at the inn, she'd experienced a feeling of tranquillity in Reece's arms. Now the possibility of finding real serenity seemed remote at best.

She didn't know how long she stood there, her cheek pressed to the rough trunk of the tree. When she finally regained her bearings, she made her way through the darkness to the inn. What she needed, she decided, was a good grounding in reality to jolt her back to her senses.

An idea formed in her mind to put a call through to Paris on the off chance that she could locate her aunt. A heart-to-heart talk spanning several thousand miles was not an ideal solution, but it would have to do.

After a bit of searching, she found a phone in a dim corner of the lobby. She picked up the receiver to dial the operator. Thoughts of her aunt's matchmaking tendencies made her reconsider. What if Aunt Tisha delighted in the notion that Callie was attracted to the manager of Casa de la Rosa Blanca? Would she be able to resist playing the role of Cupid's helper and listen with a sympathetic ear to her niece's concerns?

And just what are my concerns? Callie asked herself. *I'm not in love with Reece Tanner, am I?*

Just as the operator came on the line, Callie hung up the phone. Whatever her feelings were for Reece, she would sort them out herself.

Callie walked aimlessly around the lobby for several

minutes, stopping to look at the titles of the books on the bookshelves without really seeing them.

An hour later, she lay in bed, listening to the distant rumble of thunder. She hadn't bothered to turn on a lamp in her room when she'd gone upstairs. All she'd wanted to do was crawl under the covers and shut out the world.

Her head swam with indecision. Should she pack her bags in earnest and cook up some hasty excuse for cutting her vacation short? Or should she try to forget what had happened between her and Reece and tough it out for the next three weeks with a firm resolve to keep her contact with him to a bare minimum?

The memory of his kiss blazed in her mind. She blamed her fatal romantic streak for her brief lapse in sanity. It had been frighteningly easy to con herself into thinking that the dance they'd shared under the moon had been a moment out of time. But if she were truthful, she'd have to admit that she'd seized the moment as eagerly as had Reece.

Why had she asked him if he believed in destiny? Did she harbor some crazy idea that destiny had brought her to the inn—and to his arms? She thought about the *campesino* and Laurel, and the diary that Reece said had been found in the very room she was occupying.

Maybe he had made that up. Had he used similar ploys to get other single female guests into his arms?

Callie couldn't buy her own line of reasoning—that Reece might only have been playing with her heart. All the signs were that he had been hurt by something or someone in his past. Hadn't Ada Hawk declared as much? Callie was growing more and more convinced that Ada was an astute judge of character. She was also more certain than ever that Reece kept his life a closed book to those he met.

She understood. Some hurts were too painful to share with others who were apt to put on a show of pity—or worse, offer irritating platitudes. Then why did she yearn to open the closed book of Reece Tanner's life and peek inside?

She tossed and turned between the sheets, plumped her pillow, twice rose to straighten the covers that had become mussed from her inability to find a restful position. Finally, exhausted, she fell into a fitful doze.

A loud crack snapped Callie from her sleep. She sat up in bed to the sound of her heart slamming against her ribs. The pounding of her heart seemed to signal an impending panic attack. Then she saw a streak of lightning through the windows and rain splashing against the panes of glass. Thunder shook the walls of the inn. The wind made an eerie wailing sound through the courtyard.

Callie stared into the darkness. Even the candle in the wall sconce had burned out. Another bolt of lightning lit up the sky, illuminating the room as bright as day. Callie gasped, her eyes fixed on the far wall. There, suspended in the blackness of night, was the painting of the white rose.

Chapter Six

T he next morning at breakfast Callie asked Elena about the painting of the white rose.

"Mr. Tanner said he thought you would enjoy having the picture in your room, and so I hung it in a spot where you could see it each morning when you waken." Elena set a platter of blueberry pancakes in front of Callie. "Have you heard how Casa de la Rosa Blanca came by its name?"

Callie unfolded her napkin and laid it in her lap. "He ... Mr. Tanner told me the story of the *campesino* and Laurel." A feeling of warmth crept into her cheeks at the heady remembrance of the dance they had shared under the moon, the glory of Reece's kiss. She glanced out the window and saw the brilliance of the morning, fresh and new, as if the desert had been scrubbed clean by the storm that had wakened her in the night. A part of her felt fresh and new as well. Anticipation blossomed in her heart and made her think that perhaps it wouldn't take as long as she'd believed to find the courage to fall in love again. Or was she harboring an illusion—like the shimmering desert mirage that teased dying souls with a promise of respite, only to vanish before their eyes?

"You said you've lived in the Sonoran a long time, Elena," she said at last. "Did you know the *campesino* or the Mallorys?"

"No. I was born west of Rio Puerco and spent most of

my life there. Before I came to Casa de la Rosa Blanca, I cooked and kept house for a rancher and his family, who have a spread near the Papago Indian Reservation.''

''I heard music playing the first night I was here—and last night too. Re—Mr. Tanner said it's the *campesino* playing the 'Sonoran Love Song.' ''

Elena laughed. ''The 'Sonoran Love Song'? I believe that Mr. Tanner has made up a bit of romance for your sake, Miss Townsend.''

Embellishing the story, in other words, thought Callie.

''But the music is lovely just the same,'' Elena went on. She lifted her gaze to the window. ''He plays for reasons that only he knows, though I suspect he plays to please others as much as himself. And who am I to say that his music is not a love song, if others wish it to be so?''

''Neat hat.''

Callie smiled at Marcos. ''Thanks. How do you like my new boots?'' She hitched her jeans legs as far as her ankles.

Marcos leaned over for an inspection. ''Wow!'' He gave a low whistle. ''Tony Lama!''

''How can you tell?''

'' 'Cause Mr. Tanner always buys Tony Lamas. He took me to town with him once when he got a new pair. I think they cost a *lot* of money. How much did yours cost?''

''Very little money. I got them on sale.'' She noticed the plastic water jug strapped to the back of Marcos's bicycle. ''I even brought my own canteen.'' She'd been right in guessing that Elena would supply her with cold water, and when the housekeeper had learned that her guest was headed to Vulture's Creek with Marcos as her guide, she'd packed treats too—along with a warning to be careful. ''And Elena sent along some granola bars.''

Marcos brightened. ''Cool!'' He frowned at the camera slung on a strap around her neck. ''What kind of camera is *that?*''

"My trusty Nikon. I plan on snapping a few pictures of Vulture's Creek. So how about taking me there?"

"Sure." He propped his bicycle against a nearby tree and unfastened the water bottle. "I guess we'd better walk, since you don't have a bike."

"Good idea, Marcos. Lead on."

They wove their way through the oasis and crossed the creekbed at a spot where there was a small trickle of water. Marcos picked up a smooth, speckled stone and tried to skip it on the water, but it landed instead with a plop in the sand. He shrugged and moved on. At the spring, he paused to dip a brown hand into the water for a drink. Callie followed suit. The water tasted cold and sweet.

"There's the corral," he said after they finally emerged from the trees. He ran toward a fence-off area that was bordered on one side by a small barn. Half the corral was a faded gray color, the other spanking white.

"Is this the fence you and your grandpa are painting?" Callie asked when she caught to Marcos.

He hopped up on the railing and hooked his legs around a board. "Yeah. Good job, huh?"

Callie smiled. "Very good job. Mr. Tanner said he'll be bringing the horses back down from the summer pasture soon. Do you and your grandpa go with him?"

"Grandpa used to, but he says he's too old now. I got to go last year. Maybe you could come along," he added with a child's uncanny sense of timing.

"I doubt that I can, Marcos."

"Why not? Mr. Tanner sure could use the help," he said very seriously.

"He'll have you, won't he?"

"Probably. If I'm not in *school*."

"Don't you like school?"

"Yeah, it's okay."

"I'll bet you get good grades."

He leaped from the railing to the ground. "Four *A*'s and a *B* last year," he said with a flash of winning brown eyes.

They walked down a dusty trail that snaked through a forest of aging saguaro. Many were no more than bleached skeletons, decaying remnants of once-hardy plants. Yet even in death, the saguaro exhibited a certain dignity and elegance. Callie wondered if Reece found them beautiful too, as he did the "walking rain" and the jumping cholla.

She gave Marcos a granola bar to eat while she snapped shots of the saguaros against a background of cloudless sky.

A small bird flitted in and out of a hole in one of the dying plants. Before Callie could adjust the lens for a close-up shot, the bird darted into its hiding place again.

They moved on toward the mountains. The terrain became less flat, with rises and gullies, and the ground was dotted with an abundance of delicate, lacy-looking plants made up of bare silver-green stems. A distinctive odor permeated the air.

"What's that smell?" Callie asked.

"Greasewood." Marcos pointed to one of the several-foot-high plants. "Mr. Tanner says the proper name is creosote and that when it rains, the creosote gives us nature's perfume. But I think it's yucky."

Callie wasn't so sure she'd call the strangely medicinal scent either *yucky* or *nature's perfume*. But she didn't find it unpleasant.

"There's Vulture's Creek!" Marcos pointed at the horizon from the small hill where they stood.

Callie saw nothing except a thin line of trees in the distance. "How far?" she asked. A feeling of tenderness worried the flesh of her right big toe where it rested against the inside of the boot.

"Maybe two miles. We'll go by way of the arroyo."

"Arroyo?"

"Yeah, it's a shortcut. But Grandpa Aguilar told me never to walk in an arroyo when there's a storm," he said as they dipped down into a depression cut between two ridges.

"Why not?"

" 'Cause I'd get washed away like Mrs. Ratchet and Squeaker, an' they wouldn't find my body until after the arroyo dried up."

An occasional puddle dotted the bottom of the arroyo, reflecting blue sky. A small gray lizard slithered away from one of the puddles as Callie stepped over it. "Who were Mrs. Ratchet and Squeaker?"

"Grandpa said she was a squatter, an' Squeaker was her pet pig. They lived in one of the old houses at Vulture's Creek. She had lots of chickens too, an' she always walked in the arroyo with a big stick to fight off the rattlers. Then one day there was a gully-washer an' Mrs. Ratchet and Squeaker got drowned. An' that's how Rio Puerco got its name, 'cause they found Squeaker's body washed up by the town. But they didn't find Mrs. Ratchet till a long time later, an' there was nothing left 'cept her bones and her shoes." He made a face, then grinned.

Callie smiled, but her mind flashed back to grim thoughts of Nolan floundering in the waters of the small, isolated lake on the outskirts of Milwaukee. Had he fought for air as Mrs. Ratchet must have fought? Or had he slipped without protest beneath the icy surface because it was his intention to die there? She glanced toward the Sierritas. A band of dark clouds snagged the mountaintops, portending a lightning show and downpour later.

It seemed to her that they came upon Vulture's Creek all at once. The ghost town was nestled close to the hills and skirted a grove of cottonwood and other trees.

Following Marcos under an odd arrangement of wooden posts that fashioned a sort of welcoming gate, Callie got her first impression of the humble adobe buildings that made up the abandoned community.

Her heart gave an excited leap as she viewed the town. There were perhaps eight buildings altogether, in various stages of dissolution. A few had corrugated-metal roofs and windows that were boarded over. Most stood open, eroded by an endless parade of wind, sun, and rain. A rusted sign hung at a crooked angle above one of the sturdier buildings. Greasewood and ocotillo and a few saguaros grew up around the town. One particular tall saguaro caught Callie's fancy; it was bent forward so that it appeared to be spying through an empty window.

"Do you think Vulture's Creek is called a ghost town 'cause nobody lives here but ghosts?"

"No," she said thoughtfully. "I believe it's called a ghost town because all the people left a long time ago."

"Everyone says the mine's haunted, an' if you come here at night a spook'll catch you by the pants an' drag you down the mine shaft. I'm not scared of ghosts," he declared.

"Do people say that because Mr. Tanner found a dead man in the mine?"

"Maybe." Marcos picked up a small chunk of crumbled adobe from the ground and gave it a swift toss toward one of the buildings. The chunk hit the side of the structure and exploded in a shower of dust over a crooked metal railing that at one time might have skirted a porch. "Want me to show you the mine?" he said.

There wasn't much to see, only a partly boarded-up hole pitched against a hillside and remnants of a wooden scaffold that leaned forward at a precarious angle. "What kind of mining did the men do here, Marcos?"

"Silver. Grandpa told me there's still a vein fifty feet down that's worth *millions* of dollars. When I grow up and get out of school, I'm going in and mine the ore," he said with confidence. "You can look in if you want. It's safe 'cause Mr. Tanner boarded it up."

Callie stared between the boards into pitch blackness. The smell of must and dank earth met her nose. "If the mine's so deep, how did Mr. Tanner find the man's body?" Her question echoed loudly along the shaft until it was swallowed by the darkness.

"Grandpa said the dead man was hanging half over a shelf of rock. Mr. Tanner saw his feet an' pulled him out before he fell—whoosh!—over the edge. Pretty cool, huh?'' Marcos beamed.

Callie summoned a smile. "Yes . . . pretty cool," she said. A vision of Reece dragging the man's stiff body out of the treacherous black depths gave her a queasy feeling.

She stepped gingerly away from the shaft. The discomfort in her right toe where it rubbed against the boot was growing decidedly worse. Not only that, the outside of her left foot and both heels throbbed. She tried to ignore the notion that blisters were forming in those places as she concentrated on resetting the aperture size on her camera.

"What are you doing?"

"Adjusting the diaphragm to a daylight setting. See? A camera is like your eye, Marcos. At night the pupil of your eye gets larger because there's not much light available to help you view things clearly."

"And in the daytime, my pupil gets smaller," he put in, "since there's lots of light to help me see stuff."

"Exactly. So I'm making the aperture—or pupil—of my camera smaller. Then I can take sharper, clearer pictures of all the neat buildings here."

"Will you take my picture?"

"I'd love to."

She took a photo of Marcos standing in front of the mine shaft, then posing beside the scaffold. He started to clamber up on the boards—"so I can pretend I'm going to jump off," he said—but Callie nixed the idea as far too risky. She made up her mind to wait for a serious photo shoot of Vulture's Creek until she could return on her own. Marcos was a great kid, and she couldn't deny she was growing fond of him. But she could see that he would prove to be a distraction to her desire to poke around the old mining camp and preserve it on film. Not only that, the pain in her feet was beginning to interfere with her ability to walk. She should have heeded Reece's warning about breaking in the boots.

Marcos jogged ahead on the path down from the mine. ''Why're you walking funny?'' he asked, backpedaling.

Callie grimaced. ''I'm afraid I'm getting blisters on my feet. I guess I should have been a little more careful and worn them around the inn for a while.''

''Uh-oh.'' He gave a dramatic shake of his head. ''One of my sisters got blisters on her feet, and she couldn't put shoes on for a whole week.''

Real encouraging, Callie thought.

They sat on a large boulder under a tree and drank from their canteens. Then, with a last, longing glance back at Vulture's Creek, Callie limped at a snail's pace beside Marcos. She comforted herself by reasoning that the prospect of returning to Vulture's Creek gave her a viable reason for staying on at the inn—and a distraction to keep her mind off of Reece.

By the time they reached the corral, Callie could barely drag one foot in front of the other. Each step was an exercise in torture.

''Mmmm,'' she gritted between pressed lips. ''Why don't you go ahead, Marcos.'' She braced herself on the fence. ''I'll be along in a few minutes.''

A frown furrowed his smooth brow as he appeared to study the matter. ''You'd better wait in the barn, an' I'll get Mr. Tanner to rescue you.''

Great. Just what I wanted, for Reece to come and see me in my death throes from wearing my new boots to Vulture's Creek. ''I don't need—'' she began, but Marcos was already on his way. ''Marcos!'' she called after him in vain.

She had little choice except to hobble into the barn. It was either that or fry in the sun. Though the barn was stiflingly hot, at least it offered shelter, and there were a couple of bales of hay piled near a stall where she could sit and put her feet up.

She'd just finished the last of the water in the canteen and was testing her weight on her aching feet when Reece loomed in the doorway.

"What do we have here?" he said.

The twinkle in his eye rankled her. She looked past him. "Where's Marcos?"

"I sent him on. I'm confident I can handle this situation on my own."

"What situation?" she asked, knowing full well.

"This." He reached down and scooped her up in his arms. "All right," he commanded, "put your arms around my neck."

Her protest that she could walk under her own power, thank you, died on her lips, and she meekly slid her arms over his broad shoulders.

"You're as light as a leaf in the wind," he said in a voice that was more tender than tough.

She rested her cheek against the smooth, cool cotton of his shirt and tried to dismiss the idea that she fit perfectly in his arms. Nolan had never lifted and carried her as Reece was doing now. When she thought of it, she realized there'd never been a reason for him to.

Callie closed her eyes and didn't open them again until Reece pushed open the door of the inn. He deposited her on one of the sofas in the lobby and laid her camera aside.

"I hope you've learned a good lesson," he said, "and gotten your fill of that ghost town."

His rebuke stung worse than the pain in her feet. But if he thought he could intimidate her, he was in for a surprise. She lifted her chin, ready to fire off a saucy reply, when he pivoted on his heel and left the room. By the time he returned, carrying a towel and a basin and a small leather bag, she'd made up her mind that the smart course was to say nothing to him at all about Vulture's Creek, since she had every intention of doing as she pleased when it came to visiting the ghost town. She'd just have to exercise a measure of caution and use her common sense on future treks.

"I'll have to remove your boots, Callie," he said in a far gentler tone of voice. "This may hurt a little."

"I can take it." She clamped her mouth shut and watched as Reece kneeled beside her. He eased the boots off with a deft, smooth touch and guided her feet into the basin. The lukewarm water had a pleasant aromatic smell.

"We'll soak your feet."

"What kind of concoction are my feet soaking in?" She saw for the first time the angry welts raised on her toes and around her heels.

Reece smiled. "A recipe that Doc Stoner inherited from a Tohono O'odham Indian chief."

"Tohono O . . ." Callie stumbled on the name.

"O'odham," Reece repeated with a grin. "It means 'desert people.' They were once called the Papago."

"Elena mentioned the Papago Reservation."

Reece nodded. "The Indian chief shared the tribe's herbal remedy with Doc Stoner after he'd saved the chief's wife and baby girl in childbirth. The remedy works wonders on boils and blisters and sunburn."

After her feet had soaked for a time, Reece unzipped the bag and removed a small bottle of clear liquid, several cotton balls, and what looked like a wickedly sharp sewing needle. "We keep a first-aid kit for emergencies. Like this one," he added with another smile.

His bedside manner was impeccable, Callie had to admit.

"Hmm," he said as he lifted her left foot from the water and patted it dry with the towel. He proceeded to probe along the side of her heel with his fingers, avoiding the blistered area.

"What's wrong?"

"It looks like you might be forming a heel spur."

"What are you, Reece Tanner—a doctor?" she joked.

His eyes darkened. "Anyone who's had a heel spur can learn to spot one easily enough," he replied crisply. "Believe me, they can be mighty painful."

"Well, since you're something of an expert—"

"Who said I'm an expert?"

"You seem to know a great deal about heel spurs. So what do you recommend I do?"

"What I did. Pay a visit to an orthopedic specialist when you get home."

He finished up with her feet, pricking the worst blisters with the pin that he'd sterilized with alcohol from the bottle. Then he took some bandaging material from the kit and cut it in pieces.

"Moleskin," he explained as he fashioned a doughnut-like hole in each piece and fitted the pieces over the blisters. "Your feet should be fit to walk on in a couple of days. In the meantime I'd advise you to stay out of those boots and rub this on your heels and toes before you slip your shoes on." He handed her a can of talcum powder. "Or you could play stubborn with me again. You seem to be good at that."

"I'm sure it takes a stubborn person to know one," she retorted. And maybe a lonely one too, she decided as his eyes locked on hers for a heartbeat. His hand lingered on her ankle, and it seemed to her that there was the touch of a healer in those warm, strong fingers.

"Just what was your profession?" she asked softly. "That is, before innkeeper and sculptor."

He lowered his eyes and made a small adjustment to one of the bandages. "I was, as they say, a jack-of-all-trades. Carpenter. Painter. Roofer. Let's see." He shrugged. "Had my own landscape business for a time."

Encouraged that he'd opened up to her a little, she asked, "And where were you a jack-of-all-trades?"

"Seattle mostly." He raised his head. "Are you always so full of questions?"

She looked at him squarely. "I've learned that at times it pays to be nosy."

His mouth curved up on one side, but there was a cold quality to his gaze. "And I've learned that at times it pays to mind my own business."

"In any case," she said, striving to keep her tone light, "I say you'd make a wonderful doctor."

Reece barked a laugh. "Reece Tanner, M.D." He snorted. "The great healer? No, Callie. I'd just as soon leave the practice of medicine to capable people like Evan Stoner."

"Still, I confess that I think you have a terrific bedside manner."

He sobered and leaned closer, until his breath heated her lips. "Is that so?" he whispered, framing her face in his hands.

Staring up at him, Callie had the uncanny feeling that the two of them were drawn together by a common, desperate thread, each seeking something from the other, yet unable to say exactly what it was or where it might lead them.

Reece's mouth hovered above hers. Then without warning he pulled back. A look of confusion glazed his eyes before he turned away and rose stiffly to his feet.

His back to her, he said, "I'll have Elena fix up the basin for you in the morning so you can soak your feet again." He paused. "You'd better go on now and get ready for dinner."

With a stab of longing, Callie watched Reece leave the room. Where was the man who had proclaimed that he believed in living in the present? How did he manage to stir so many contrary emotions in her? She was soothed by his presence one moment, then disturbed the next. The dreamer in her was helplessly attracted to him, wanted so much to trust him, while the voice of reason shouted loud and clear, *If you know what's good for you, you'll steer clear of Reece Tanner for the rest of your vacation!*

How could she remotely entertain the thought of becoming romantically entangled with a man whose moods had a way of changing like quicksilver? Callie pushed the question aside as she rose from the sofa and tested her ability to walk. The Indian remedy and Reece's moleskin pads had worked a near miracle on her feet. She could navigate with-out wanting to scream in pain with every step.

She picked up her camera case in one hand and her boots in the other and made her way across the lobby. She heard a din of conversation coming from the dining room—a man's voice, harsh and nasal, then a woman's answering in shrill, loud tones.

Callie remembered that Elena had said guests were due in from Chicago. At the time she had looked forward to meeting them. A burst of hearty laughter convinced her she wasn't up to a dose of humor that evening. So she crept away and wearily mounted the stairs. A couple of leftover granola bars would have to suffice for dinner.

Wonderful aromas greeted her when she opened the door to her room. Her spirits revived a little. On the bureau sat a silver tray laden with covered dishes. Callie shook her head and smiled as she went to see what Elena had prepared for her. Her footsteps halted when she saw the single white rose nestled against the pillow on her bed. Momentarily forgetting her hunger, she picked up the rose. A bead of moisture clung to one of the creamy petals. The drop of water cooled her flushed skin when she pressed the rose to her cheek. The petals perfumed the air with a sweet scent that reminded her of dancing under a starry sky.

In a dreamlike state, she walked to the window, opened it, and gazed down. Shadows stretched the length of the courtyard through a deepening purple twilight.

In the gathering dusk, Reece stepped out from behind the statues of Romeo and Juliet. As if he knew Callie was there, he raised his head and looked toward the window. In the instant that their eyes met, a volley of thunder rum-bled across the far hills like the cracking report of gunfire.

Chapter Seven

" "And then I sold the dealership in Skokie and bought up a Buick showroom in Oak Park. Profitable little deal, that." Fred Peloskie pulled a cigar from the pocket of his shirt. He put it in his mouth and chewed on it briefly, then took it out and laid it on the table beside his plate. "Manager told me I couldn't smoke in here," he said with a scowl. "Said it was against the law."

Thank you, Reece, Callie thought. It had been enough to endure Fred Peloskie's bragging, let alone have to breathe in a haze of cigar smoke. She'd quickly learned that Fred had a monstrous ego when he and his wife, Edy, had invited themselves to share her table at lunch.

"Hard to break away from the job," he said with a cough. "Lots of pressure, you know, but we gotta have a vacation, be good to ourselves now and then."

Callie realized that all the things Fred Peloskie represented were the very things she had come to the desert to forget. And to make matters worse, Fred bore an uncanny resemblance to Stu Lutz, one of the senior partners in the law firm back in Milwaukee.

Lunch with the Peloskies was a jarring contrast to the quiet morning she'd spent in her room. Elena had brought her breakfast on a tray along with the basin of water to soak her feet. The herbal remedy had worked wonders on the blisters, and after a dusting of talcum powder on her

81

heels and toes, she'd been able to wear her shoes with minimal discomfort.

A mention of the blisters was all it had taken to set Fred off on a tirade against the health care system in America.

"Nothin' but a blasted racket, that's what it is," he'd groused. Then he'd launched into what Aunt Tisha called an "organ recital," plying Callie with tales of his operations.

After learning the function of the shunt the doctor had inserted in Fred's right side following the removal of his gallbladder, Callie lost her appetite and made a quick retreat to the lobby with the book on ghost town under her arm. Unfortunately, the Peloskies came traipsing after her and settled their portly frames in chairs opposite hers.

"Ah, this is the life," Fred proclaimed with a wink at Callie.

Edy raised her eyes a notch from the book she was reading and scowled at him.

Fred shot a narrow glance at his wife and leaned toward Callie. "So you're from the city of brats and brew."

She forced a polite smile. From the size of Fred's stomach, it appeared he enjoyed more than his fair share of both brats and brew.

"I've got a heavy bet riding on the White Sox besting the Brewers this year," he went on. His bushy eyebrows wiggled. "Of course, I don't suppose a dainty young thing like you would care much about baseball."

The hair at the back of Callie's neck prickled. "Oh, not much. But I do recall the year Ricky Bones won a staff-high ten games. Wasn't that the same year the Brewers beat the White Sox three games straight with Reyes, Bones, and Wegman on the pitcher's mound?"

Fred's mouth dropped open, and he shook his head. "I'll be a—"

"What's wrong? Dainty young thing got your tongue?"

"Shut up, Edy," he said with a snarl. His face flushed the shade of a ripe beet.

Edy whooped a laugh instead, and the color in Fred's cheeks deepened to purple.

Callie feared she was about to witness the war of the Peloskies. She was ready to bolt the scene when Fred broke into hearty guffaws.

"Shoot, Edy," he said, wiping a stream of sweat from his brow, "you're right." He turned to Callie. "Sorry, miss. I had it coming. Edy's been reading me this book lately—*Men Are from Mars, Women Are from Jupiter.* and—"

"That's Venus," Edy cut in.

"Whatever." Fred shrugged his massive shoulders. "Anyway, just chalk my comment up to the gender gap and"—he grinned—"heck, I s'pose I still want to think of women as these pretty little fainthearted things that like to be petted and pampered."

"Fred Peloskie!"

He put up his hands. "Okay. Okay. I give up, Edy."

Callie was almost beginning to pity the obnoxious Fred. But not enough to confess that she wasn't quite the avid baseball fan she pretended to be. Or to bring up the disturbing fact that it was Nolan Jamison who had drummed those statistics into her head.

There was a lull in the conversation after that. Edy went back to her reading. Finally Fred hefted himself from his chair and strolled over to the bookshelves. That gave Callie the chance to extricate herself from their company. She went outside in search of quiet and ended up in the oasis. She spent the afternoon in one of the hammocks, reading the section about Vulture's Creek in the book on ghost towns. As Marcos had said, the mines at Vulture's Creek had produced rich veins of ore. At one time the town had a population of nearly three thousand and boasted two banks, six saloons, a barbershop and funeral parlor, and a first-class hotel. The town lost two-thirds of its residents when the veins grew thin. According to the book, the death blow to Vulture's Creek came when a flood of water and mud slides rushed in on the town after a violent thunder-storm. Twenty people lost their lives, and only a dozen buildings were left standing after the wall of water receded.

Callie thought of Marcos's story of Mrs. Ratchet and Squeaker and of Reece's caution that the desert could be deadly as well as beautiful. His warnings didn't dampen her determination to return to Vulture's Creek, but she couldn't deny that her respect for his advice had climbed a few notches in the past couple of days.

As she read, she found herself listening for the *chink* of Reece's hammer and chisel against stone. But only silence greeted her ears, except for the excited call of a bird from some high branch of the cottonwood tree.

After a while the wind died away completely, and even the tree-shaded hammock failed to provide a comfortable respite from the sweltering heat. Callie mopped beads of perspiration from her cheeks and brow with a tissue she'd found in her shorts pocket. Finally she gave up and sought out the dim, cool depths of the inn.

"This is the hottest it's been in many weeks," Elena remarked as she set a mixed green salad in front of Callie at dinner. "Almost a hundred at noon in Tucson, according to the weatherman on the radio."

Fred Peloskie snorted. "You want hot? Last time we were in Arizona it was so danged hot, you could've fried a lizard on a rock and had him for breakfast." He dug his fork into his salad and brought a heaping bite to his mouth. "Isn't that right, Edy?"

Edy rolled her eyes heavenward and heaved a sigh. "Every year it's the same story with Fred. He complains about the heat." She waved a forkful of greens in her husband's direction. "And where does he say we're going on our vacation? The desert! Tell me, now, does that make sense?"

Elena exchanged glances with Callie and telegraphed a sympathetic smile her way.

Throughout the evening meal, Callie endured another

round of "Peloskie's platitudes and complaints" as she'd labeled them in her mind. When he launched into a tirade about the deplorable state of air travel in America, she began to long for the solitude of eating alone in an empty dining room.

"And there we were, in San Francisco, left out in the pouring rain, with nothing on our backs but our shirts and our shorts. No coats. No umbrellas. Blasted airline lost every stitch of our luggage!" He slammed his fist down on the table.

Callie jumped—and nearly dropped her water glass.

"Simmer down, Fred!" Edy reached across the table and thumped her husband hard on the arm. "You're scaring the young woman to death. Not to mention boring her silly."

"Aw, Edy," he said in that appeasing tone he seemed to employ when his wife was upset, "you're at it again." He set sad, bloodhoundlike eyes on Callie. "Now tell me I've scared you, miss, or bored you, and I swear you won't hear another word cross these lips of mine."

"No . . ." Callie took a fast swallow of water. "Of course you didn't." *Chicken!* she cursed herself, wishing she were anywhere but there.

Apparently her assurance was just the signal Fred needed to launch into his rules on childrearing.

"Give em' the willow switch for punishment. Stings like heck. Raised our sons on the willow switch, love, and hard work. Both had paper routes through their school years. The older one, Bob, is an electrician, set up his own business. Got married last June, and he and his new bride are ready to start a family. I just bumped Ray—he's our youngest, fresh out of college, just got engaged—to assistant manager of the dealership."

Fred leaned back in his chair and regarded Callie. "I'm surprised a pretty young gal like you isn't married. Bet you've had plenty of chances. Guess the right one hasn't come along yet, huh?"

"Fred, how could you?" his wife scolded. "Young

women these days have careers *and* relationships. They don't *have* to get married and be chained to some man for the rest of their lives.''

Callie stared past both of them, a smile fixed on her face. ''If you'll excuse me.'' Evading Fred's gaze for fear of finding those bloodhound eyes tracking her, she mumbled something about seeing them at breakfast.

''Didn't I tell you you'd drive her away with your nosy questions and loudmouthed—''

Callie missed the last of Edy's tirade as she fled the dining room and sought refuge in the courtyard. There was a new crispness to the air. Callie drew in a cleansing breath and stretched her arms over her head to ease the tension between her shoulder blades.

The sweet strains of the *campesino*'s music drifted over the dusky stillness, a welcome balm to Callie's ears. She glanced around, half expecting, half yearning for Reece to step out from the shadow of one of the statues. Instead, Elena appeared at the door of the inn and came to join her.

''Ah, he's playing for us tonight,'' Elena said.

Callie followed Elena's gaze to the section of the inn fronted by the porch. The windows under the long porch were dark, as usual.

''Those are Mr. Tanner's quarters,'' the housekeeper offered. ''He is gone overnight to Phoenix. All of these are his sculptures.'' Her sweeping gesture took in the garden. ''He's a talented man, intelligent as well. But I think that sometimes he—'' She stopped abruptly.

''That he what?'' Callie prompted.

''It's nothing really.'' She shook her head. ''None of my business, of course. But I'm curious why a young man like him would want to live here, in a place where there are so few people, and why he is alone without a wife and children.''

I'm curious too, Callie almost confessed, *and I wish I didn't want to know.* She thought of the Peloskies' skewed ideas about marriage and wondered if she were in danger of one day becoming jaded, like Edy.

Elena lifted her face to the sky. "The temperature is going down. I can feel in the air that autumn will be here soon. Fall is the time for fires every evening in the hearth and extra blankets on the beds." She smiled. "I must get back to work now. Enjoy the music," she said and turned to go inside.

Callie stood for a while, listening, remembering how wonderfully free she had felt dancing in Reece's arms under stars that burned across the black band of night.

Why was he in Phoenix? She imagined the desert city, with its dazzling lights, congestion, and noise. Like any other city, she supposed, in many ways. Like Milwaukee.

Why should I care what he's doing in Phoenix? she asked herself.

In a matter of weeks she would be leaving Casa de la Rosa Blanca and Reece behind. When she returned home she had important decisions to make. The biggest was whether to quit her job, find other employment that was less demanding—even if it meant a cut in pay—so that she would have the time she wanted to devote to her photography.

Soon, she consoled herself, *thoughts of Reece Tanner and the Sonoran Desert and its legends will be nothing but a pleasant, hazy memory.*

Who was she deceiving? A verse from the Bible sprang into her mind, one that she had read on a snowy afternoon not long after Nolan's death. Its truth had shaken her then. It unsettled her now.

"The heart is more treacherous than anything else, and is desperate. Who can know it?"

Was it mere fascination that drew her to Reece, pure physical attraction that made her pulse pound at the sight of him? Or was it something more? A flicker of hope welled deep inside of her that here was a man she might fall in love with if she gave herself half a chance. And if circumstances were different, she reminded herself. Even then, could she trust her heart to make the right choice?

The concert came to an end, and Callie could find no real reason to linger in the courtyard. As she walked toward the inn, she saw a moonlit reflection of herself, flanked by the tragic figures of Romeo and Juliet, in one of the darkened windows.

That night Callie tossed in restless dreams of Nolan and Reece, of Romeo and Juliet and other statues magically brought to life under the wide Sonoran sky. The statues held white roses in their hands as they surrounded her, circling and chanting words she couldn't understand. They closed ranks and hurled the roses at her feet. Their chanting grew louder, more insistent, until Callie cowered in their presence, caught like a frightened bird in a trap.

Callie wakened with a cry. She remembered the strange nightmare in its entirety. "Beware," she said under her breath. Was that what the statues had been trying to tell her—to beware? Of what? Of the dangers lurking, unseen, in the desert? Or of a hidden danger, one that was more lethal than the sting of a scorpion or the swift strike of a rattler because, after all, it involved her heart?

Familiar feelings of anxiety gnawed at her nerves. Then she heard angry voices, and she laughed in relief.

The Peloskies, she thought. Their room was just down the hall. Their bickering must have wakened her.

The din died down as quickly as it had flared. Callie got up and went into the bathroom for a drink of water. The candle in the wall sconce was still burning, and she glanced up at the painting of the white rose as she passed. The pearly white petals, the waxy green leaves and stem looked so lifelike, she was tempted to reach out and touch them. Ironically, the real rose she'd found on her pillow the night before was already losing its petals, even though she had tried to preserve it by placing it in a small vase Elena had provided for her.

On her way back to bed, Callie paused at the window to reassure herself the statues below were all in their appointed places and that her dream had been the product of an overactive imagination fueled by the Peloskies' midnight sparring match.

The courtyard looked serene and orderly, but as Callie gazed down, she sensed that something was out of place. While she was trying to figure out what bothered her, a man emerged from around the statue of Balzac, and she knew what was different. She'd seen the partial silhouette of the man beside the statue.

Instantly she knew the man couldn't be Reece. The figure was slightly built and a little stooped. Besides, Reece was in Phoenix.

The man was carrying something in his hand. A shaft of moonlight revealed a row of silver strings stretched taut to the long neck of a guitar. Callie's heart accelerated. She pressed closer to the glass in an attempt to glimpse the man's face. But he suddenly wheeled and vanished behind the statue of the countess like a shadow accustomed to playing hide-and-seek with the night.

Chapter Eight

The next morning, rather than face the Peloskies over breakfast, Callie stood by the window munching on leftover granola bars and staring out at the spot where she'd glimpsed the *campesino* in the moonlight. Frustrated and restless, she barely tasted the strawberry-flavored bars as she thought of lovers made of cold granite, and of couples whose wounds ran so deep they might wish their hearts would stop beating and turn to stone.

Callie got out her camera and went downstairs with the purpose of taking some shots of the ocotillo and other strange succulents that inhabited the inn's garden. She saw Elena in the lobby bent over a table, a feather duster in her hand.

"Miss Townsend! I thought you weren't coming for breakfast this morning." The housekeeper straightened and tucked the duster in her apron pocket.

"Actually, I've already eaten."

An eyebrow shot up. "Eaten what?"

"Leftover granola bars," Callie confessed with a sheepish smile.

Elena clucked under her breath. "That is not a breakfast. Now come into the dining room," she ordered.

Mercifully for Callie, the Peloskies were nowhere in sight. She sat down at her usual table and didn't protest when Elena served her a generous portion of scrambled eggs and home-fried potatoes.

"How are your feet today?" Elena asked. She placed a compote of fresh fruit on one side of Callie's plate, a cup of coffee on the other.

"Much better. Just about healed, in fact." Wearing her comfy Rockports, she hardly noticed the tender spots on her toes and heels.

"Good. Mr. Tanner was quite concerned about you."

Callie stopped in the middle of slathering jam on a piece of toast. "Was he?"

Elena smiled down at her. "I would not think you'd be so surprised," she said before turning to leave.

As Callie was finishing her meal, the housekeeper came back to refill Callie's coffee cup.

"Mr. and Mrs. Peloskie have gone to lie in the hammocks, I believe," Elena said.

Callie made a mental note to avoid the oasis and dallied for a while over her coffee.

The rest of the morning passed quickly for Callie. She used up the roll of film in her camera and returned to her room for a fresh roll. Still sated from breakfast, she skipped lunch, choosing instead to curl up on one of the sofas in the lobby with the book on ghost towns. When she tired of reading that, she selected a yellowed paperback novel from a bookshelf. The inn was quiet, the novel dull, and Callie's mind drifted from the words on the page to her conversation with Elena at breakfast.

Reece was concerned about her. Elena wouldn't have said it if it wasn't true, would she? A warmth spread through Callie, chasing the numbness, the dark shadows of doubt that had stalked her since Nolan's death. Then she remembered the way Reece had pulled back from her after he'd finished the task of bandaging her feet; instead of kissing her, as she'd expected, a look of confusion had clouded his face. Her sense of calm was again shaken like still waters disturbed by the dropping of a stone. As she fell into a doze, the chill stole back into her body and the shadows returned.

The sound of loud chatter startled Callie awake. She peeked with one eye as the Peloskies lumbered through the lobby, wearing identical lurid flower-splashed shirts and tight red shorts. For a moment Callie feared that Fred and Edy were going to plop their ample posteriors onto the cushioned chairs that flanked the sofa. She pretended to snooze until she heard the pair's voices begin to fade away. The slamming of a door in the upstairs hallway signaled that the coast was clear, and she let out a grateful sigh.

She steeled herself for the couple's company at dinner, but they didn't show. She ate alone, for once savoring the solitude. She was finishing her dessert of crème brûlée when she looked up and saw Reece standing in the doorway. Surprised and pleased, she couldn't help staring at him as he strode to her table. Clad in beige slacks and a neatly pressed white shirt, he looked more the savvy businessman arriving for a weekend getaway at a classy resort than the manager of a little-known inn whose only amenities were two hammocks and a hot tub.

"I thought you were in Phoenix," she said, hating that her voice held a slight tremor.

"I was." His mouth crooked up at one corner. "But I'm glad to be back." He placed his hand on the table next to hers. "I hear your feet are on the mend."

"Much better—thanks to your treatment."

He glanced toward the courtyard. "I'm going to check on the horses tomorrow. You're welcome to come along if you'd like."

"I'd like to," she said before she could convince herself of some reason to refuse.

"If you packed a sweater or jacket," he said without looking at her, "bring it along. It'll be considerably cooler in the mountains than here, and there could be a rainstorm. The monsoon season's been running late this year."

* * *

They left shortly after nine the next morning. Elena had filled a basket for them with sandwiches and fruit and a jug of iced tea. Callie toted her camera and the light jacket that she'd decided to stuff into her suitcase at the last minute.

As they rode down a straight paved road toward the mountains, Reece pointed out more marvels of the desert— spiny yucca plants and Parry's agave that looked more lethal to Callie than any jumping cholla; a jackrabbit that streaked across the road in two powerful bounds and disappeared under a scrub oak tree; a rattler sunning itself at the edge of the tarry pavement.

"I see you brought your camera," Reece said.

Callie smiled. "I rarely go anywhere without it." She told him of her futile attempts to photograph the tiny bird that made its home in a dying saguaro.

"That's a cactus wren." He swung the van onto a dirt road that was little more than a crooked trail blazed through the sand. "Let's see what we can do to accommodate you and your camera."

He pulled up beside a small stand of decaying saguaro and they got out. "This way." He took her hand and led her to a tall cactus that was pocked with numerous holes.

They stood, patiently waiting until a wren appeared and perched itself at the entrance to one of the holes.

Callie trained her Nikon on the pretty brown-and-white-speckled bird. The wren flitted away, then just as quickly returned to the hole. All the while it squawked at Callie in a scolding tone.

"The cactus wren's one of the loudest, most contentious birds in the Sonoran," Reece said. He folded his arms over his chest. "Reminds you of some people. Now its cousin, the canyon wren, is the opposite. Polite, a bit shy, with a melody so sweet, seductive, it's guaranteed to send shivers up your spine."

Just hearing Reece tell about it sent a tingle along Callie's back. "Like the 'Sonoran Love Song,' you mean?"

Reece's eyes met hers. "Exactly the same."

She half expected—hoped—that he would reach for her hand again. He didn't. But as they walked back to the van, Callie was conscious of Reece matching his steps to hers.

Closer to the mountains, the arid terrain gave way to hills that were flecked with scrub oak and, here and there, dense patches of vegetation.

"It doesn't take a whole lot of rain in the desert to green things up," Reece remarked. He shifted the van into a lower gear as the road began to steepen. The engine choked once. After that the van took the grade without further protest, and Reece deftly negotiated a series of hairpin curves that took them higher into the mountains.

Callie looked out the window at a sheer drop of hundreds of feet to the desert floor spread out below. For a breathtaking instant, she had the sensation that the van was suspended in midair.

"I hope you're not afraid of heights."

"I'm not," she assured Reece. That was one thing she'd never feared. "I was always the one who climbed the highest trees."

"Were you?" He smiled. "So was I."

Callie hoarded the scrap of information and tried to visualize in her mind the carefree boy Reece once must have been. "Sometimes I was lonely," she said, gazing out the window, "because I didn't have brothers or sisters to climb trees with." She paused a moment. "Did you?"

"No."

The tight answer, spoken in a cold tone, dimmed Callie's hopes that he might have decided to open up to her.

Then he surprised her by saying, "I had a brother, two years older than me. He died of leukemia when I was five, so we didn't have much chance to climb trees—or do anything else—together."

She looked at him. "I'm sorry. I had no idea."

He stared straight ahead. "Of course you didn't. A few years after that, my parents divorced. My father ended up in Canada somewhere. He'd write me postcards, send gifts once in a while. Finally he quit writing altogether. My mother was killed in an auto accident when I was twenty.''

''You have no other family?''

''No.''

''My parents were divorced too,'' she said quietly. ''And my dad died when I was a teenager.''

The hollow, detached quality in his voice when he'd told her about his family, and his glum profile, told her more loudly than words that he was still profoundly affected by his father's desertion and the deaths of his brother and mother. Callie didn't wonder that Reece would withdraw into himself, make the conscious choice to live alone. Yet she couldn't dismiss the niggling thought that there was more to his story, other reasons for his aloneness that he chose not to share with her.

''How did you happen to come to Arizona?'' she asked.

He didn't respond at once as he negotiated a hairpin turn. ''In large part, curiosity. I was thumbing through a magazine one day and came across an ad for the inn. I decided, What the heck, might as well bum around down there for a while. When I got here, I found out they were looking for help, so I hired on.''

''Was there anything in particular that convinced you to stay?''

''Just the solitude of the place, I guess.''

His hands gripped the wheel and he clamped his jaw shut, discouraging further conversation. Callie took the hint and looked out the side window, conscious of the heavy silence inside the van.

When they came to a fork in the mountain road, Reece took the right branch, a densely rutted dirt trail that introduced them to more level terrain and sturdy stands of trees whose branches at times rose to form a leafy tent over them.

The van bucked and jolted along the road for a few more miles. Callie was surprised that Reece didn't switch on the radio and let a soulful country song drown out the silence. Maybe the van's radio couldn't pick up SNOR's signal at that distance. Or maybe Reece just liked things quiet for a change.

"We're almost there," he said at last.

A moment later Callie spied an opening through the trees, a sea of green and amber grass that was hemmed in on three sides by bare rocky outcroppings.

Reece pulled up beside a gated fence and they got out of the van. He unlatched the gate and motioned Callie through. Putting his fingers to his mouth, he gave a loud whistle.

Callie strained to spot two roans and a mare. "I don't see any horses. Could they have gotten loose?" The fence, she noticed, looked none too sturdy.

"Patience," Reece said, and whistled again.

Out of nowhere, it seemed, one of the geldings appeared, nickering and bobbing its head as it trotted up to greet Reece. Its reddish coat gleamed in the sun. A cool breeze ruffled its russet-colored mane.

"Hello there, Moonfire," Reece said softly. "How have you been, boy? Where's Princess and Bo?"

Callie watched Reece's fingers work through the coarse hairs of Moonfire's mane, and she thought of the possessive way they'd tangled in her hair, the tenderness with which they had bandaged the blisters on her feet. A stab of longing seared through her—a longing for his touch, but more than that, to gain his trust because perhaps then she too would find the courage to trust again.

"Moonfire's as gentle as a lamb," he said. "You can come closer."

Callie moved forward and reached out to pat the gelding's nose. "Moonfire's nose feels like velvet," she murmured.

"Mmm-hmm. But it wasn't always like that."

"What do you mean?"

At that instant the other two horses cantered up to Reece.

Both horses were as sleek and beautiful as Moonfire, though the mare was smaller than the geldings.

Reece went to the van and returned with several carrots. ''This one's for Princess.''

Callie took the carrot he held out to her. ''Come here, Princess,'' she called.

A little thrill of satisfaction shot through her when the mare ambled over and snatched the carrot from her hand. ''Good girl,'' she crooned as Princess nuzzled her palm. ''I think she's hinting for another one.''

Reece chuckled. ''Later, after we've had our own lunch. We don't want to spoil her too much.''

Callie wiped her hand on her jeans. ''As you were saying about Moonfire's nose.''

''Moonfire, Princess, and Bo were one of the main attractions in a traveling carnival,'' he said, hitching one booted foot up on a slat in the fence. He gazed at the horses. ''The outfit was putting on a performance in Yuma. Someone noticed the poor condition of the horses and called the local Humane Society. After an investigation, the owner of the show was cited for cruelty to animals. He lost the horses and was slapped with a heavy fine. Moonfire, Princess, and Bo were put up for adoption. Carlos—that's Marcos's grandfather, by the—''

''Marcos told me.''

Reece smiled. ''I figured he had. Then you're aware too that Carlos works at the inn. At any rate, he heard about the horses from a cousin who lives near Yuma. Henry Bennett wrote out a check to pay for the critters, sight unseen, and so Carlos and I went over to Yuma in a couple of borrowed pickup trucks, pulling two horse trailers. It's taken a considerable amount of TLC to restore the horses to a decent state of health. But we made it, didn't we, Bo?''

The gelding neighed and licked Reece's hand. Reece took the time to scratch Bo's ear before continuing.

''Moonfire had welts on his nose and back. All three

horses were half-starved and showed signs of being whipped.''

Callie shuddered. ''I hate people who abuse animals!'' she blurted.

''I can't abide them, either,'' Reece agreed stonily. ''No more than people who abuse or take advantage of other people.''

His declaration hit Callie with all the force of storm clouds darkening the sun. Tears sprang to her eyes, and she turned away.

The next instant Reece's hand was on her arm. ''What's wrong?'' he asked.

''Nothing.''

''If it's nothing, then why are you crying?''

Callie swiped at the wetness on her cheeks. ''I'm not crying.''

Taking hold of her chin, he made her look at him. ''What's this?'' He tracked the path of a tear with his finger.

''It's just—'' She drew an unsteady breath. ''I have a tender spot for animals and—''

''No!'' he interrupted. ''It's more than that, isn't it, Callie?''

His gaze locked on hers and she began to tremble. She noticed that he held his hands rigidly at his sides as if he were waging an inner battle with himself, and she sensed that he wanted to take her in his arms, draw the truth from her by the persuasion of his touch, his kiss. Under his scrutiny, the protective barrier she'd erected after Nolan's death to guard her heart began to shatter like a fragile vase that had been dealt a hammer blow.

''I was betrayed,'' she said, voice cracking, ''by the man I was going to marry. Only I didn't know what he had done until after he—'' She swallowed back the tightness in her throat. ''Until after Nolan died.''

Reece's mouth thinned into a grim line. ''What did he do to you?''

Callie looked up at the sky. A cloud was racing toward the sun. "We met through mutual friends. For a while we were casual acquaintances; we'd see each other in passing at parties, wave hello or good-bye and that was all. Then he asked me out, and within a year we were engaged. I thought we would marry, have a long, happy life together." She shook her head.

"Tell me."

"Nolan was the chief loan officer at the largest bank in Milwaukee. He owned a penthouse condo and drove a fancy sports car. I assumed that his salary gave him the freedom to spend money as he pleased—though it bothered me that he felt the need to surround himself with so many things. But he was generous with me, and we had plans to build a house in a secluded area near our favorite lake." She drew in a shaky breath. "It was the lake where . . . where Nolan drowned."

She was aware that Reece had closed the small distance between them. His arms came around her, and she felt the whisper of his mouth across her cheek. "Go on," he urged.

The rest of the story poured from her lips. Of her initial shock and denial on learning of Nolan's death. Of how his drowning was officially declared an accident. Of how in the week following his funeral she'd been dealt a blow by the stunning news that he had been head over heels in debt because of gambling bets and risky investment ventures. Of how she'd reeled under the revelation that shortly before his death his supervisor had confronted him with evidence that Nolan had been embezzling funds from the bank.

"And what else?"

Reece's voice was flat and cold, but his fingers were warm as they stroked a strand of hair away from her brow.

"His secretary discovered that he was stealing from certain accounts. Apparently he'd started an affair with her before we got engaged, then broke it off. She must have been as greedy as he was because she threatened to blackmail him if he didn't share the money with her."

"There's more, isn't there?" Reece coaxed.

A bitter laugh escaped her. "Nolan not only stole from the bank. He withdrew funds from our joint savings account. It was the money we'd planned on using for our new home—a home we hoped to one day fill with children. Or at least I had hoped," she finished in a whisper.

Reece's hold on her tightened. "When did this happen?"

"A year ago . . . thirteen months."

"That's not long."

"I've asked myself a thousand times why I didn't see that something was horribly wrong," she said more to herself than to Reece. "We argued about the hours he was putting in at the bank. I thought he was working. . . ." She shook her head. "The last few months before he died, he . . . At times I would ask him a question, and he wouldn't respond. He would just drift off. I chalked it up to pressures at work, his preoccupation with plans for our future. I was worried—for all the wrong reasons."

Reece shook her gently. "Callie! You couldn't have known. You don't believe his death was an accident, do you?"

"I don't know what to believe!" Her voice trembled with anger. "Nolan's supervisor said that he begged him for another chance, and that Nolan had sworn he'd never meant to steal from the accounts, only borrow, but that somehow it had all spiraled out of control and . . ." Her hands curled into fists and she began to shake.

Reece simply held her for a time, rocking her, rubbing her back until the shaking ceased. He didn't offer smug advice or spout clichés. He didn't tell her to just forget the past because she couldn't change anything, and for that she was grateful.

"So you came to Arizona to escape the hurt for a while?" he asked.

His intuitive question made her eyes misty again, and suddenly she began to feel as if she had been in a black tunnel trying to grope her way out, and Reece had pointed her toward the light.

"My doctor thought it would help me to heal," she said.

"Well, now that you're here, how would you like to learn to ride a horse?" He turned her to face Princess. "It isn't as hard as it might look, and Princess is a fine, obedient mare."

Princess came and gently nuzzled Calie's hand.

"I think I'd like that," Callie said.

"I'll help you on."

Her eyes widened. "Now?"

Reece grinned. "Can you think of a better time?" He motioned her over to the mare. "Here. Grab a hunk of mane and I'll give you a boost up."

She did as he instructed, and he took hold of her waist, lifting her onto the mare's back.

"Hang on tight," he warned.

Reece led the mare in a slow circle near the fence, with Callie clutching the rough hair of Princess's mane in a death grip. Shortly Moonfire and Bo joined the procession, flanking Princess like dutiful bodyguards.

As she got used to the feel of sitting astride the mare, Callie began to relax and take note of the beauty of the high mountain meadow clad in early autumn's brightness.

The landscape unfurled like an artist's canvas of green and gold and pink with bright swirls of lavender and red mixed in for bold contrast. The air was faintly perfumed with the sweet odor of flowers blended with the heady smell of grass. Where the floor of the canyon met the rock walls, shadows played along the high stony crevices. The echo of birdsong bounced off the canyon rims.

An unaccustomed feeling of joyfulness welled inside Callie until it burst forth in exuberant laughter. A look of surprise registered on Reece's face. Then his mouth relaxed in a smile and he began to laugh too.

"Sometimes," she said, "I guess we have to be willing to take a chance in order to see the world from a different perspective.'' And she liked this particular perspective, with Reece standing beside the mare, sunlight angled on his face. She noted for the first time the fine lines etched around his eyes and the corners of his mouth, the sprinkling of silver hairs among the thick sable strands.

Princess plodded along obediently behind Reece, following him to the gate. When they stopped, Reece reached up to hoist Callie off the mare.

''How'd you enjoy your lesson?'' he asked.

''Very much,'' she admitted.

Reeece's arms stayed at her waist for a moment. His breath burned a trail on her cheek, and she froze, her body wedged between Reece and the mare's left flank.

Her heart gave a lurch as Reece's hands slipped up to her arms and came to rest on her shoulders. He pulled her around to face him.

''Callie—''

Her name on his tongue was beguiling, a smooth caress. She stood, mesmerized, as his thumb traced a slow path across her chin. His fingers whispered down the curve of her neck.

''I believe in living in the present, Callie. It's all we have.'' The truth of what Reece had told her before rumbled through her as his eyes riveted on hers. Then his mouth took hers in an urgent kiss, and she couldn't think beyond that moment of ecstasy she'd found in his arms. The past was gone; she couldn't relive it. The future was uncertain, a question mark in her mind. All that mattered to her now was standing in a sun-dappled meadow, locked in an embrace with a man she hadn't known existed a short time ago.

Is this how love should be, she wondered as he deepened the kiss, *a dizzying carousel ride that makes me so giddy with pleasure that I toss common sense to the wind?*

Then Reece broke the kiss, and the carousel careened to a sudden stop. He drew a ragged breath, and she willed her own breathing to slow to a normal pace while he held her a heartbeat longer.

He touched his forehead to hers. "We should eat our lunch," he whispered.

"Yes," she agreed shakily, unable to imagine how she could get her legs to move, much less summon an appetite for the food Elena had prepared. Somehow she managed to put one foot in front of the other and walk with Reece to the van, where he retrieved the picnic basket.

They found a spot under a spreading sycamore tree, and Callie discovered that she could eat her sliced turkey sandwich after all. Cups of sweet iced tea poured from the jug washed down the sandwich and yummy cole slaw and homemade brownies.

Callie eyed the few crumbs that were the only remains of her meal. "I didn't realize I was that hungry." She smiled at Reece, who was leaning against the trunk of the tree, his legs stretched out in front of him. The couple of yards separating them, and their preoccupation with the food, had given her the time she'd needed to examine her emotions in a more rational light.

She couldn't deny her burgeoning attraction to Reece, but she must not allow herself to think it could ever be more than that. He had made her feel desirable; she'd needed comfort, and he'd been obviously willing to oblige. Maybe that was what he'd needed too. Once her vacation was over she'd be gone, and he would resume his usual routine—carving couples out of stone and whatever else it was that he did as keeper of a run-down inn. She would resume her life in Milwaukee—whatever that was or would be. Her eyes met his, and she imagined he was thinking that too.

"The Bennetts should promote Elena's cooking in their advertisement for the inn," she said. "I must've gained five pounds at least since I came here."

"Five pounds or twenty-five. You'll only be more beautiful, Callie."

Her face suffused with heat, and she made a pretense of watching the horses graze nearby on shoots of tall grass. In a flash of recollection, she realized that Nolan had rarely flattered her with a compliment.

She had believed that she'd understood Nolan so well when she hadn't known him at all. He had talked at length about himself, whereas Reece was silent or used an economy of words to make his point. Nolan had never hesitated to share his opinion on any subject with anyone who was willing to listen. Reece shared his opinions judiciously—if at all.

A sharp ache of regret stabbed at her heart, and the shining loveliness of the day seemed to lose its luster. The air suddenly turned chill too, forcing her to shrug into her jacket.

"Come on." Reece held out his hand to her. "Let's feed the horses their carrots. Then we'll walk off our lunch."

They returned the picnic basket to the van and left Moonfire, Bo, and Princess happily munching on their carrots.

Reece chose a trail that ran beside a gurgling stream.

"How'd you get interested in photography?" he asked.

Callie paused to adjust her Nikon for a close-up shot of a purple many-flowered plant he'd identified as a Gilia.

"My parents gave me a play camera when I was six," she said. "After they noticed I seemed to have a decided compulsion for snapping a picture of anything that crossed my path, they bought me my first real camera. I was eleven then. Photography's been a passion of mine ever since."

"Have you ever thought of making it a career?"

Callie smiled. "Actually, I have," she revealed. "I guess I just haven't had the courage to give up the security of my day job for the uncertainty of freelance photography." *At least not yet,* she almost told him, *but that might change one day if Gunther Graham likes the photographs I plan on taking of Vulture's Creek.*

"And what is your day job?"

"Administrative assistant to four overworked and understaffed attorneys."

"I see." Reece grew quiet. "Sometimes," he said after a moment, "you have to choose to make the sacrifice, take a chance, and strike out in a new direction. If you don't, you might not be given that chance again."

Callie slid a glance at him as they moved on. "What about you? How did you get into sculpting?"

"I started out, as most kids do, with Play-Doh, making dinosaurs and monsters and aliens from outer space."

She laughed, and Reece grinned. "Seriously?"

He held up his hand. "I swear. In high school I graduated to more serious mediums like clay, and later still to stone. I've stuck with stone, though I tried my hand at woodcarving once or twice."

"No advanced training after high school?"

"I've taken night courses now and again at a community college."

"You're very good. And your subject matter is . . ." She groped for the right word to describe the pairs of couples he'd preserved in stone. "Intriguing," she said.

"Thanks," he replied.

And you're modest too, she thought, suspecting that he wasn't aware of how much talent he possessed. "Haven't you ever dreamed of one day seeing your statues on display at the National Gallery or maybe the Louvre?"

It was his turn to laugh. "The Louvre? Aren't you aiming a bit high?" He paused to pick up a tiny, glistening piece of rock and study it. "I suppose I've had an idea or two of getting a bid on my work from some well-known gallery," he said, tossing the rock aside.

"Have you ever had a show?"

"That's one of the reasons I went to Phoenix. Besides picking up a load of supplies for the inn, I had an appointment with the owner of a gallery there. He agreed to take several of my smaller sculptures for his spring show.

Look.'' He pointed to a ground squirrel that was perched on a ledge.

"How adorable!''

"You'd better aim your camera quick or he'll be gone.''

Callie fumbled in her haste to focus the Nikon on the tiny creature. But she still managed to snap a picture before the squirrel skittered off.

By the time they made their way back down the trail, she had used up most of the film she'd brought with her. She'd purposely saved the last few frames for pictures of the horses.

She stopped at a distance from where Moonfire, Bo, and Princess were grazing. After adjusting the aperture on the lens, she snapped a wide-angle shot of the meadow with slender shafts of sunshine backlighting the horses.

Reece went on, and Callie observed him as he stroked each horse in turn and talked to them. Suddenly he took hold of Moonfire's mane and mounted the gelding. Callie saw a chance too good to pass up.

"Wait!'' she called, rushing toward the horses. She feared that Reece was going to take off on the gelding across the meadow before she had a chance to capture him on film. She came to a halt just short of Moonfire's nose and bent her head to check the shutter speed on the camera.

In the next instant, she felt the hard grip of Reece's hand on her arm.

"What do you think you're doing?'' he demanded.

"Isn't it obvious?''

Reece's eyes glittered with anger. "Don't you know the sound of that camera can spook a horse?''

"I—'' Her mouth fell open. She was too stunned by his anger to respond. Then her own temper flared. "Why didn't you tell me?'' she snapped, twisting from his grasp.

"I would've thought you'd have guessed as much.'' He spun on his heel and started away from her.

"Why would you think that when I don't know anything about horses?'' She hurled the question at his back.

He didn't answer. Only when he'd reached the gate did he slow his steps and wait for her to catch up.

She whipped past him without a glance and marched toward the van. His hand on her shoulder stopped her.

"I was wrong, Callie."

She'd been ready to fire off a sharp reply, but the humility in his voice made her swallow her words.

He shook his head. "I shouldn't have expected you to know how easily a horse can be spooked at times."

She felt suddenly very tired. "It's okay," she said, but she couldn't bring herself to look at him. Settled in the van, she stared out the window, hoping for a last glimpse of the horses. But what she saw when she lifted her eyes were dark thunderheads building over the canyon walls.

Chapter Nine

That night Callie stood staring out the windows in her room, listening to the wind sing through the empty court-yard below. Despite the thunderheads veiling the mountains in an armor of heavy, dark clouds, the desert floor had received very little rain, a mere sprinkling.

Though she'd taken a soak in the hot tub, her whole body ached with exhaustion. Maybe her weariness was due to the strain of having to endure another round of the Pelos-kies' company at dinner. More likely it was because the ride down from the mountains with Reece that afternoon had been fraught with tension. After his abrupt apology for lashing out at her attempt to photograph the horses, he had tossed out a few innocuous remarks and then clammed up.

Once they were settled inside the van, he had resorted to his usual tactic of turning on the radio, and a string of sad country songs about love gone wrong had once more substituted for conversation on the way back to the inn.

Was Reece so embarrassed by his show of anger that he hadn't known what else to say beyond "I'm sorry"? she wondered as she gazed down at the statues. Was the flare of temper just further evidence that he was enigmatic and given to moods? Or was he so bitter over the circumstances of his life, so grieved by his losses, that his misery was bound to spill over and color his dealings with everyone he came in contact with?

She no longer questioned that he had a gentle side. In the meadow he had sensed her disquiet and tactfully drawn her out until she found herself sharing with him the sordid details of Nolan's betrayal.

But Reece was able to do far more than coax stories of heartbreak from her lips. He had the gift of making her laugh—even at her own foibles. And he had the undeniable power to stir emotions in her that she'd begun to believe might never be wakened again.

Would he ever reveal more of the circumstances of his life than the few crumbs he'd tossed out to her that afternoon? She would be fooling herself if she denied that the chemistry between them was strong. But was she naive enough to think that she could stand so near the blaze now and hope to contain the flames of desire the moment she boarded the plane for home?

A single jagged streak of lightning lit up the sky above the courtyard. Callie cranked open the window a few inches to see if she could detect the scent of rain as Reece declared he was able to do. The air coming through the crack was torrid and smelled of dust—nothing like the humidity-charged atmosphere that hung heavily over the city of Milwaukee on steamy summer nights. Any hint of fall and cool evenings seemed to have fled the Sonoran Desert.

She heard the soft splashing of water in the fountain, an echo of thunder. That was all.

A few minutes later Callie lay in bed, her gaze focussed on the painting of the white rose. It seemed that no matter where she was in the room, she had a clear view of the painting. As she closed eyes that were heavy with sleep, another, more disturbing notion intruded on her thoughts. No matter where she was at any given minute of the day— the inn itself, Vulture's Creek, a flower-strewn meadow high in the mountains—she had a clear view of Reece Tanner in her mind.

*   *   *

"And where are we off to today?" Elena asked as she set a plate of eggs and toast in front of Callie.

Callie fiddled with her fork. "I thought I'd spend some time in the oasis and do a bit of exploring."

"You're going back to Vulture's Creek perhaps?"

Callie glanced up into Elena's round, inquisitive eyes. Did those guileless eyes possess the ability to see through the fabric of her jeans pocket to the map of Vulture's Creek she had tucked there? While hastily thumbing through the book on ghost towns that morning, she'd happened across the map in the appendix.

"So then," Elena went on, "is Mr. Tanner going with you this time?"

"No, not exactly."

The housekeeper frowned. "Don't tell me you are planning on going to that place alone?"

Callie straightened. "Yes, I am."

Elena pursed her lips, seemed to ponder the matter. "I think it would be better if you didn't, but who am I to say what a guest can or cannot do?" She raised her hands in a helpless gesture. "So I will prepare a canteen of water for you."

By the time Callie left the inn, she had her camera hung around her neck, the canteen slung across her shoulder, and a hefty snack of sandwiches and fruit stashed in her knapsack. She wore her straw hat and a thick layer of sunscreen. Her one quandary had been over whether to chance trying the new boots again, since her feet were healed. She'd come to the conclusion that she'd rather risk the fangs of a rattler splitting open her Rockports than another bout of painful blisters.

She closely followed Marcos's route to the ghost town. At the bubbling spring she scooped a handful of water to her mouth, but the taste of it didn't seem as sweet to her tongue as when Marcos had been with her.

Approaching the corral, she noticed half the fence was still spanking white, the other half faded gray. Farther on she passed through the forest of dying saguaro. Their decaying trunks looked more desolate than ever, their bare, bleached limbs stretched toward the sky.

As she walked along the arroyo, she saw water pooled in shallow puddles and deduced that it must have rained hard in the mountains the night before. She thought of Mrs. Ratchet and Squeaker and the warning Carlos Aguilar had given his grandson about avoiding an arroyo after a storm.

Callie's steps slowed at the gateway to Vulture's Creek. The jumble of buildings that lay before her presented a forbidding picture, and she could understand how a pilgrim of old might have felt after traveling many miles in search of paradise and finding instead a vision of Hades. Scorched by the relentless sun, the ruins of Vulture's Creek reminded her of a graveyard of broken dreams.

She took the folded map from her pocket and consulted it. The task served a twofold purpose. One, it quelled the jangling in her nerves that she suspected came from being utterly alone in a desolate place. Two, it helped her orient herself in relation to the scattered remnants of the mining town.

She walked with a certain vigilance, wary of a sneak attack by a rattler or giant spider or other critter of unknown origin and danger. With a glance toward the rickety scaffolding perched on the hill, she recalled Marcos's assertion that there was a vein of silver in the old mine ''worth millions of dollars.'' Had the man whose body Reece discovered been chasing a dream of riches? Had he let down his guard and sought out the mine, only to have his hopes take a disastrous turn when he stumbled into the tunnel and met his death?

Callie turned her gaze away and made herself concentrate on the map instead of on dead men. Comparing the layout of the buildings on the map with the adobe shells that were still standing, she took an educated guess as to which had been destroyed by the mud slide and flood and which had survived.

Most of the saloons, which the map showed had been lined along the south side of the town's main street, were gone. The bank too, and numerous cabins that had housed the miners and their families, were buried in the silt.

But the livery, which Callie deduced was situated on the other side of the street, had been spared. She saw the crumbling remains of the structure as she looked north. Beside the livery stood the two-story shell of the Silver Lode, the town's once-glorious hotel. There was a space overgrown with weeds and cacti between the hotel and the next building, which had housed the combination barbershop and funeral home. The shop sported the crooked sign that had caught Callie's attention on her visit with Marcos.

She approached the shop to see if she could find any lettering on the sign. There was nothing that was readable, just dabs and streaks of yellow and blue paint speckling the rusted metal. She snapped a picture of the sign, then walked to the livery to frame a shot of the saguaro that appeared to be spying through a vacant window.

She took a moment to peruse the map again in an attempt to identify more of the shambles. One roofless structure, she guessed, had housed the bawdy Birdcage Saloon. Beyond that she wasn't certain of the rest, so she tucked the map back in her jeans pocket, not caring to waste precious minutes that could be better spent in exploring the town.

She started by taking a couple of wide-angle shots of the remains of Vulture's Creek. Then she photographed each of the buildings in turn. But her real interest lay in discovering fascinating details that might be overlooked by the casual visitor.

She spent some time scouting around the exterior of the buildings. She discovered a thicket of scrub oak, sycamore, and brush a couple hundred or so yards beyond the back wall of the Silver Lode. She made a mental note to check it out later. According to the map, the cemetery should be in the general area of the thicket.

Running her fingers over a portion of wall of the old

hotel, she noted the texture of the adobe, that it was rough and pocked with holes in places, while smooth and seamless in others. She peeked through a paneless window in the livery and stared into near darkness. When her eyes had adjusted to the lack of light, she realized that the interior was illuminated by softly scattered sunshine that poked through rifts in the metal roof.

The view of the inside of the old livery was almost ethereal. For a moment Callie had the distinct feeling that she was trespassing, stepping over a boundary into a place where outsiders—or even ghosts—weren't welcome, and where scorpions and spiders now held sole privilege of occupation.

She took a picture through the window frame as dust spun and swirled like fairy fire down the shafts of sunlight. She stood on the threshold and imagined she saw a weary traveler leading his horse across the dirt floor to a roomy stall bedded with straw.

Something scurried in front of her toes, and she let out a cry. She shivered, imagining the creature was a hairy spider. She remembered her declaration to Reece that she wasn't afraid of spiders, but as she proceeded cautiously, she wasn't so certain anymore that her bravado extended to tarantulas the size of saucers.

A slightly fetid smell permeated the close air. Callie made herself believe that the odor came from the rotting remnants of the wooden stalls—not the carcass of some animal that had crept into the barn to die.

The clack of the shutter on her camera resounded time and again through the empty building as she took pictures of twisted gray slats basking in sunlight and the rusted remains of an old anvil that she happened upon.

When the atmosphere in the livery grew too oppressive, Callie retreated to the sunshine outside and paused to down several swallows of water from the canteen. A coating of perspiration slicked her brow and upper lip.

Good thing I'm by myself, she thought, lifting the hem of her shirt to dry off the beads of sweat.

Just then a gust of wind set the leaves of a sycamore tree rattling. Callie cast a glance over her shoulder. Had her idea of being alone suddenly roused the bones of some long-since-departed soul and incurred his sense of humor?

Another good thing, she reminded herself as she moved on to the barbershop and funeral home, *is that I don't believe in ghosts.* Then it dawned on her. There were ghosts in Vulture's Creek. They just weren't human. They were the battered buildings, whipped and worn down over countless years by the elements but not quite conquered. Something about their gaping, windowless frames suggested pride and the feeling that they might yet come out the victor in the endless war waged on them by wind, rain, and sun.

Callie felt a twinge of regret that she hadn't brought along her journal to record her impressions of the mining camp before they were distorted by time and distance.

Inside the barbershop she found a treasure trove of mementos from the past. A topsy-turvy barber chair. Shards of colored glass—blue, white, and green—strewn here and there on the buckled wooden floor. Three brown bottles, empty but intact, lined a surprisingly well-preserved metal shelf. A jar with the letters *cr* readable on its side stood beside the bottles.

A mirror hanging crookedly on a wall had just enough shine on its surface to reflect back to Callie a distorted image of herself.

At one side of the shop a door led into another room. A shudder raked up Callie's spine as she peeked through the doorway into darkness. The odor of must and rotting wood assailed her nose. She turned away, trying to ignore the fact that the room had once served as an embalming parlor.

She expended more effort and more film in photographing the inside of the barbershop than she had intended to. She played with the bottles, setting them along a window until she found a spot where sunlight shone through them like amber-colored fire. She tilted the chair into an upright position, only to have it wobble crazily in the next instant and topple over. On her third attempt, she succeeded in getting the picture she wanted before the chair went crashing with a thud onto the floor.

By the time she emerged from the building, she was tired, drenched with sweat, and had a raging thirst. She lifted the canteen to her lips and drank greedily from it.

"Hi."

Callie jumped. "What—" She sputtered, coughing on a swallow of water. She spun around. "Marcos," she said weakly between gasps. "What are you doing here?"

He grinned up at her. "I'm on my way to help Grandpa finish painting the corral." He thrust his hands into the raggedy pockets of his jeans.

Callie took a deep breath and collected her wits. She wasn't used to mischievous little boys sneaking up on her in the middle of a ghost town. "Aren't you supposed to be in school?" She looked at her watch. "It's only quarter past twelve."

"They're having parent-teacher conferences today, so we got out before lunch."

Parent-teacher conferences. She could buy that. "Do you always come through Vulture's Creek on your way to the corral?"

He scuffed the toe of his boot in the dirt. "Nah, just when I want to take a shortcut." He eyed her camera. "Did you get a picture of the ghost in the mine?"

Callie fought to conceal a smile. "No, but I took a few shots of its haunting grounds."

"Cool." Marcos glanced around. "You want to come with me? You can meet my grandpa."

She looked at the sky. While the sun blazed overhead, clouds skimmed the rise of the highest hill. No use risking sunstroke—or a flash flood in the arroyo if the clouds brewed up a thunderstorm. A vision swam through her head of Reece finding her body in the arroyo, her bones picked clean by birds of prey, with only tatters of her clothing left for identification. *"Silly woman,"* he would as he stared at her skeleton. *"So this is what you get for not listening to me."*

Callie gave herself a mental shake. *It's these tales of ghosts and a man found dead in the mine that are muddling my brain.* All the while Marcos was watching her expectantly. "Sure, I'll go with you," she said, and was rewarded with a smile. "Did you eat lunch yet?" she asked, falling into step beside him.

"Uh-huh. A sandwich and a glass of milk."

"How would you like another sandwich?"

"You've got one?"

She handed him a wrapped ham sandwich and a shiny apple.

They walked along companionably while they ate, and Callie's flagging energy revived.

"What's your favorite subject in school, Marcos?"

"Baseball," he said without hesitation.

Callie feigned surprise. "If I remember right, you told me you got four *A*'s and a *B* last year. I was positive you'd say you like math or English best."

"They're okay, I guess." He aimed his empty apple core at a barrel-shaped cactus. The tiny missile hit right on target. "Mr. Tanner's bringing the horses down tomorrow."

Callie's steps slowed. "Tomorrow?"

"Yeah. Grandpa said they're going to borrow Uncle Reuben's truck and horse trailer. I wish the teachers had conferences again. Then I'd get to go up to the mountains too." He polished off the last bite of his sandwich. "Moonfire's Mr. Tanner's horse. He told me I can come after school anytime I want and curry Bo. I'm going to buy my own horse someday, and he's gonna look just like Bo."

"After you hit that vein of silver ore?" Callie asked with a smile.

Marcos grinned. "Yeah. Then I'll buy a hundred horses."

At the spring they stopped to quench their thirst, and Callie splashed handfuls of water onto her flushed skin. As they neared the corral, Marcos rushed on ahead while Callie straggled behind.

"I'll go get Grandpa," he called over his shoulder. He scampered between the railings and ducked into the barn. In a few minutes he came running out.

"Grandpa's not here. I think he probably went to town with Mr. Tanner to buy some more paint." He kicked at a stone. "You want to hang around till they come?"

She envisioned Reece's surprise at her "hanging around," waiting for him. And she imagined him scrutinizing her bedraggled appearance and asking her where she and her camera had been. "Thanks, Marcos, but I'd better head on to the inn. I hope I get to meet your grandpa tomorrow."

Marcos shrugged. "Yeah, he should be here."

Callie waved and started off.

"Hey!"

She stopped and looked back. "Yes, Marcos?"

"I got an idea. Why don't you go to Vulture's Creek some night? I'm sure you could take a picture of the ghost then."

An uneasy feeling crept over her at the thought of poking around those empty, windowless ruins by moonlight. "I'm afraid my camera's not equipped for photographing ghosts in the dark."

"Oh." Marcos seemed disappointed. Then he brightened. "Maybe you can buy another camera, one that works better."

Callie smiled. "Maybe. I'll see you around, Marcos."

"Okay. See you around."

After a long, cool shower back in her room, Callie flopped onto the bed and promptly fell into an exhausted sleep. She woke to a view of the sky deepening from azure to purple and the realization that she must have slept through dinner. She got up, switched on a lamp, and changed into the blue bare-backed halter dress she'd bought on impulse just before her trip. Her eyes strayed to the several rolls of used film that were stacked on the bureau. She wondered if there was a place in Rio Puerco that she could trust with developing her photos or if she should play it safe and wait until she returned to Milwaukee.

Callie studied her hair in the mirror, then swept it back on one side and secured it behind her ear with a fancy silver comb that had once belonged to her mother. Why was she dressing for dinner again and fussing with her hair when her only purpose in going down to the dining room was to find Elena and beg for a bite to eat?

The inn was dead quiet as she descended the stairs. All she heard was the echo of her own footsteps. There wasn't a hint of anyone about in the candlelit lobby or any indication of activity in the dining room beyond. Maybe Elena had retired for the night, having fed Edy and Fred and with the assumption that her guest from Wisconsin had eaten dinner in town with Reece.

Callie hovered at the entrance to the darkened dining room. Should she call out for Elena or knock on the kitchen door in hopes that the housekeeper would appear?

A rustling sound in the lobby drew her attention. She tensed, preparing herself for a brush with one or both of the Peloskies. But when she turned, she saw no one, only shadows dancing and scaling the walls. Then the strains of a symphony broke the silence. It was from Vivaldi's *Four Seasons*. She recognized the melody because her aunt had given her a tape of the beautifully composed masterpiece a few months after Nolan's death.

Callie wheeled around to discover Reece standing behind her. She must have looked startled, for he laughed softly. "I thought that you were—"

"One of the other guests? They're gone. I took them to the airport in Tucson this morning."

He stepped closer, and she gazed up into his face. "I

missed dinner,'' she said, ''and was looking for Elena.''
His recklessly combed hair and the five-o'clock shadow
gracing his jaw made her wonder if he had dozed off too.
Add to that the rumpled state of his beige shirt tucked care-
lessly into his jeans, and the fact that he wasn't wearing
shoes, and she deduced he'd had a hectic day ferrying the
Peloskies to the airport. Or maybe, like her, he'd had too
many nights of late when sleep had eluded him. ''Marcos
told me that you're bringing the horses down tomorrow.''

''That's right.'' He crossed his arms over his chest. ''We
can resume your lessons day after tomorrow if you like.''

''I guess there's more involved in learning to ride than
hanging on to Princess's mane and praying I don't fall
off.''

His glance at her. ''Much more,'' he said. For a moment
he seemed to hesitate; then he looked toward the dining
room. He cleared his throat. ''I'll find Elena for you. We
wouldn't want you to miss dinner.''

How could she tell him that his presence aroused in her
another kind of hunger, one that she hadn't been able to
quell? She longed for him to stay, to keep her company.
She considered confessing that she'd been to Vulture's
Creek, of triumphantly adding that no harm had come to
her there. She wanted to share with him the excitement of
her discoveries and let him know that she wasn't finished
exploring the old mining camp.

Callie prudently held her tongue. She didn't want to risk
having her enthusiasm dampened by a burst of criticism
from Reece. But when he reached the threshold of the dining room she called out to him, not willing to let him get
away so easily this time. He stopped and turned around.

The distance between them seemed vast. ''Do you know
where I could get my rolls of film developed?''

''I'll take them into town for you. Leave them with Elena
in the morning when you have breakfast.''

''All right. Thanks.''

He stood staring at her for a moment. An expression of raw yearning drew his face into taut lines.

"Why do you have to look so beautiful?" he said softly.

She wondered if he could hear her heart beating in the momentary hush that encompassed the room. Before she could say anything, the music surged again.

"Wait here," Reece said over a soaring symphony of violins. Then he strode into the darkened dining room without bothering to turn on the lights.

Chapter Ten

That night, as she slept, Callie dreamed of the statues again. In the dream she was at Vulture's Creek, and it was night. A full moon rose like an opal in the sky.

She walked under the welcoming gate. The statues were there—Romeo and Juliet, Hugo and Drouet, Balzac and the countess—waiting for her. Somewhere in the shadows the *campesino* began to play a slow, sad tune. Callie watched, entranced, as the statues closed ranks around her. Hugo reached for her hand; she recoiled from his cold touch. Then his gaze met hers and she gasped. Reece was staring back at her from the sightless depths of the statue's eyes, and when Hugo opened his mouth to speak, the voice was Reece's.

"Trust me," he whispered.

The words echoed in Callie's mind, in her heart, and reverberated like a roll of soft thunder off the stark, mysterious hills.

The statues linked arms and formed a chain. Powerless to resist, Callie followed their silent procession. They passed the old livery, the barbershop, the Silver Lode slumbering in dark silence. The *campesino* struck up a somber march. Callie's breath came short and fast; her heart pounded like the cadence of drums in a funeral cortege as the statues wound through the thicket of trees.

A cloud suddenly blotted out the moon. Lightning

121

flashed across the sky, and the gravestones stood out like clean, white bones on a black canvas. Callie stooped beside each stone to examine its inscription. Every face was blank except one.

" 'Nolan Jamison,' " Callie read the words etched on the stone. His name froze on her lips; the blood in her veins turned to ice.

The statues murmured among themselves and shook their heads. Callie walked on past the statues, drawn by a morbid fascination to the remnants of a building in the midst of the thicket. A shadow loomed in front of her; it was the shape of a person, a man. Then it disappeared. The music died away. Callie turned to look behind her. The statues were gone. She was utterly alone.

Callie woke from the dream out of sorts and with a pulsing headache. Sunshine streamed through the windows; the cheery light wasn't enough to lift the fog of confusion that enveloped her brain. She lay in bed attempting to sort out the strange dream. She thought of hibernating in her room for the rest of the morning. Then she remembered that she was to deliver the rolls of film to Elena. Stifling a groan, she dragged herself out from under the tangled sheets, pulled on shorts and a blouse, and went downstairs.

"Are you all right, Miss Townsend?" Elena cast a worried glance at Callie.

"Just a little tired," Callie fibbed. "I think I got too much sun yesterday."

"The sun in the desert is very strong. You must take care and not wander so far from the inn next time." Elena placed a glass of orange juice on the table. "A call came for you very early this morning."

Callie perked up. "Yes?"

"It was from your aunt." Elena smiled. "She said she is in Paris. She told me not to wake you."

With a stab of disappointment, Callie asked, "Did she leave a number where I could reach her?"

The housekeeper looked regretful. ''No, I'm sorry. But she did say she would call again soon.''

Callie thanked Elena for the message. She asked for and received a light breakfast of oatmeal with yogurt and fruit. In turn she entrusted the housekeeper with the rolls of film.

After she ate, she wandered into the lobby, but the room—the whole inn—was oppressively silent. For a wild moment she imagined that she missed the Peloskies, Fred's posturing. She thought of Reece going to retrieve the horses from their pasture. Closing her eyes, she thought of how right it had seemed to be held in his arms in that high mountain meadow with the ripeness of early autumn scenting the air, and of how wonderfully comforted she had been by his words of reassurance.

Her headache abated but she felt woozy and flushed. Was she running a fever? She tried to concentrate on the titles of the books, but her eyes refused to cooperate. She regretted that Elena hadn't wakened her to take the call from her aunt.

What time is it now in Paris? Early evening? Or is it already tomorrow?

Suddenly Callie wished it was tomorrow in the Sonoran Desert, because maybe then she would be all right, and tomorrow was when Reece was to give her another riding lesson.

She climbed the stairs back up to her room and spent the next several hours alternately dozing and attempting to record her feelings about Vulture's Creek in her journal. She slept through lunch. When she woke, she discovered that the fog had lifted from her brain, and the sense of feverishness was gone. She took a relaxing bath, then went down to the dining room and ate the meal that Elena had prepared for her.

Callie sipped a second glass of iced tea. By the time she climbed the stairs again to her room, the moon had risen high over the courtyard. A knock came at her door minutes later.

"Your aunt is on the telephone," Elena announced with a solicitous smile.

Callie hurried to take the call in the lobby on the same phone she had used in her attempt to secure Beatrice's number.

"Aunt Tisha?" Her heart gave a leap of anticipation as she spoke into the mouthpiece.

"Hello, Callie, my sweet. It's wonderful to hear your voice. You sound marvelous. Have you . . ."

Her aunt's voice faded. Callie pressed the receiver tight to her ear. "I can't hear you, Aunt Tisha. We must have a bad connection."

"I said"—Tisha's voice boomed over the wire—"have you fallen madly in love with the desert yet? Oh, I'm certain you have, Callie. And isn't Casa de la Rosa Blanca the most fabulously romantic inn? Do you know," Tisha rushed on without stopping for breath, "that Beatrice speaks absolutely flawless French? We've been to the Louvre twice, Carnavalet, Sacré Couer, the Opéra. We had our lunch yesterday at a place called Cartet—a charming little bistro on the rue de Malte. Only a few tables, but such cozy touches—paneled walls, lovely damask linen cloths and napkins. We had a scrumptious meal of croûte aux morilles." Tisha gave a throaty laugh. "Speaking of food, I hope you've managed to put on a few pounds indulging yourself on those marvelous meals that Elena serves. She answered the phone this morning, you know. A charming woman and a brilliant cook."

"Yes, Elena's still here. And don't worry, Aunt Tisha, the way I've been eating, I'll probably have gained twenty pounds by the time we see each other."

"So glad to hear that, Callie. Aren't the Bennetts the sweetest couple? The perfect hosts."

"The Bennetts aren't here right now. Elena told me that Mr. Bennett's in ill health and that they're in California, where he's getting some medical treatment."

There was a gasp on the other end. "What a shame! I hope he makes a good recovery. But who's in charge?"

"A man named Reece Tanner is managing the inn for them."

"Reece Tanner. Hmm. Is he an older man, dear, like Mr. Bennett?"

"Reece—old?" She laughed softly as a vision of him flashed through her mind.

"Oh, I gather he's young and handsome then. And what about his wife?"

"Aunt Tisha, if you're wondering whether he's married, the answer is no."

"Well, dear, it sounds to me like your trip is just the medicine you needed. You see, things have a way of working out. Tell me, are you—"

A crackle of static cut off Tisha's last words. The line went dead.

Callie held the phone to her ear a few seconds longer, hoping the connection to Paris wasn't completely lost. When the dial tone came on, she hung up.

She stood for a moment alone in the middle of the lobby, with the candles glowing around her and a piano concerto of *Rhapsody in Blue* filling the silence. She should have realized that her aunt was far too chatty to engage in any type of serious discussion during a five-minute transatlantic call—even if she had felt like confiding in her. It was a good thing that fate had stepped in and terminated the call before Tisha had the chance to ask her if she had fallen in love with Reece Tanner.

"For today's ride, we'll use a saddle pad minus the stirrups. I don't imagine you'd appreciate risking saddle sores your second time out." Reece grinned over his shoulder at Callie. "Of course, you could always take a good soak afterward in a tub of Doc Stoner's special remedy."

Callie offered a game smile and watched as Reece led

Princess from her stall, where she'd been contentedly munching on her oats.

He showed Callie how to position the saddle pad on Princess's back and identified the pommel, the seat, the girth, and the stirrup bars.

"You won't need the stirrups for a few lessons." He tightened the girth under the mare's belly. "I expect that you're going to be a fast learner."

"I would expect so too," Callie said, "since I'm certain that I have an expert instructor." Earlier he had relayed a message to Callie by way of Elena, letting her know that he would be at the corral the rest of the morning, if she cared to join him there after she finished her breakfast. She'd found him in the barn, pitching forkfuls of hay into Moonfire's stall. The barn looked neat and swept clean, the corral outside all freshly painted.

Reece's welcome as he'd turned toward her had given her the impression that he was in an excellent mood. Yet she noticed that he was all business as he demonstrated how to bridle a horse and proper mounting technique.

After she had the reins and a lock of Princess's mane firmly in her left hand, Reece instructed, "Bend your left knee and balance on your right leg."

She imagined she looked like an awkward contortionist as he took hold of her ankle and calf and told her that, on the count of three, he would help her onto the mare. But the plan worked beautifully, and when Reece commanded "hup," Callie was boosted onto the saddle pad.

Reece jiggled the reins. "Slacken your hold," he cautioned. He positioned the reins in her hands so they threaded through her fingers and over her open hands. His thumb skimmed her palm, lingering there for an instant, burning a path across her skin.

Princess gave a soft nicker, and Reece squared his shoulders. "Are you ready?" he asked.

"Ready," Callie replied.

He led Princess out of the barn. "We'll walk around the

corral a couple of times. I want you to get a sense of the horse—her muscles, her movements. Just relax.''

Easy for you to say, she thought. Then she remembered how quickly she had adjusted to sitting atop Princess in the meadow. Why should this be any different? But something was different. Maybe it was the confines of the corral that made Callie less certain of herself, or the problem might be the strange feel of the saddle pad rubbing against her hips and legs. Or maybe it was her keen awareness of Reece as a man whose presence, whose merest touch and glance were starting to give her notions that maybe honor and chivalry needn't be relegated solely to some make-believe knight in the pages of a fairy tale.

"We're going to practice turning," he told her. "Lean a little as Princess goes into the turn. Don't overdo it. Stay with the mare."

Under Reece's watchful eye, Callie began to gain confidence in her ability to keep her balance on Princess.

After several passes around the corral, Reece brought Princess to a halt and ran Callie through a couple of exercises designed to put her "completely at ease astride a horse." He had her lie back on the saddle pad and stare for a moment up at the sky while holding the reins loosely in her hands. Then he instructed her to drop the reins and lean forward until her head rested against the mare's neck.

She giggled when a strand of Princess's coarse mane got stuck on her mouth. Then a fly buzzed by her nose, and she swatted it away.

Reece leaned near. "What's so funny?" he said.

"Hair," she said, holding up a small fistful of mane. "And a fly."

Reece smiled. "The hair I can take care of." He fingered back the offending strand of mane from Callie's cheek. "The fly I'm not so sure about." His gaze moved over her face. "Do you know," he said, serious again, "that your eyes are the very same color as the ocean off Long Reef at St. Croix?"

"You've been to St. Croix?"

"Once." He looked lost in thought for a moment. "It was years ago, but I'll never forget that blue-green stretch of sea. Have you been there?"

She gripped the reins. "No." Would she have been happy honeymooning on St. Croix or Aruba, as Nolan had wanted? "I prefer islands with a more dramatic coastline— like the Apostles on Lake Superior. Dense woods, waves crashing on a rocky beach, the sun setting across the bay, leaving trails of pink and gold on the lake." She laughed. "You've probably never heard of the Apostle Islands."

"No." His hand covered hers. "But now I know I want to see them someday."

She imagined she read in his gaze that he wanted to see them with her—to hold her hand as they strolled down a tree-lined path and watched foamy waves crashing on the rocky shore, to take her in his arms as the sun put on its fiery show just for them.

"You've had enough riding for one day," he said, lowering his eyes.

He led Princess back to the barn. He grasped hold of of Callie's waist and helped her down from the mare. She stroked Princess's mane while Reece uncinched the girth and lifted the saddle pad off Princess's back. Next he removed the bridle and hung it over a peg on the wall.

"Marcos told me that he and his grandfather painted the corral," she said, "and that you let him help you groom the horses."

"Marcos is a great kid, real bright. And he loves horses."

Callie was quick to detect the note of affection in Reece's voice. "I got that impression too. And I'm curious to meet the man who has such an intelligent grandson."

Reece gave Princess a nudge on the rump, and the mare walked obediently into the stall. "I'm sure you'll have the chance to meet Carlos one of these days." He rested his hands on his hips. "Will you come the same time tomorrow, Callie?"

"Yes, I'll come, if you want me to."

"I want you to." He regarded her for a moment, as if there was something else on his mind that he wanted to tell her. Finally he strode over to where the pitchfork rested against the wall. Hefting the fork in his hands, he called back, "Elena'll be waiting lunch for you." Then he loaded a mound of hay onto the tines of the fork and pitched it into Bo's stall.

Callie's days took on a cadence after that. Mornings in Reece's company flowed like warm honey from a jar. Afternoons, time passed lazily by as she curled up in one of the hammocks, reading a Tom Clancy novel that she had unearthed from a bookshelf. Evenings wrapped her in a moonlit cocoon while she strolled alone in the sculpture garden, listening to the *campesino* play his blissful tunes and casting occasional glances toward the dark row of windows under the eaves of the inn. All the while she left her camera gathering dust in the bureau drawer.

She didn't go back to Vulture's Creek, though she knew she would one day soon. She did get her new boots broken in by wearing them every morning to the corral. And under Reece's watchful eye, she gained confidence in her ability to master the art of horseback riding. Reece was patient with her, even kind, and his eyes often lit with a warm glow that made her think of a fire kindled to stave off the bitter winds of a January blizzard. She basked in that glow and in his praise of her progress in "the rules of basic horsemanship," as he called them. Laughter bubbled up from inside her with little provocation, and she felt a sense of accomplishment and satisfaction she'd rarely known apart from those moments when she was capturing some rare and exciting find with her Nikon. She came to the realization that what she'd needed all along was the very thing Dr. Simmons and her aunt Tisha had advocated—a complete break from the dull routine her life had become since Nolan's death.

But nights as she lay in bed, wide-awake, were when the doubts crept in. A persuasive voice inside her head whispered that she was enjoying herself too much, that she should be living less minute-to-minute than with the sobering idea of accepting the precious hours spent in Reece's company for what they were—lovely interludes, ones that she relished, perhaps even deserved, but ones that would too quickly come to an end.

So much about him was still a mystery, and he'd shown no inclination to share more personal information with her. Yet she'd quit thinking of him as an isolated man who generally preferred his own company to that of others. He seemed to prefer her company a lot. Though she wished he would talk more about himself, she didn't want to press him for details of his life. If he wanted to share them with her, he would. If he chose not to, did it matter all that much?

Thoughts of him were always the last thing she recalled before sleep came, but her dreams were filled with visions of statues springing to life and of ghost towns and graveyards.

By the end of the week, she was using a regular Western saddle and stirrups. Reece announced she was ready to ride on her own. He handed her Princess's tack and watched while she positioned the saddle on the mare's back and adjusted the girth.

"Good," he said. "Now bridle her."

It took Callie a number of tries and detailed instructions from Reece, but she finally succeeded.

"Princess won't do anything you don't signal her to do," he said as he mounted Moonfire. "Just remember—besides your voice, your hands are your principle means of communicating with your horse." He grinned. "You might compare it to the way people sometimes choose to communicate with each other."

Heat rose in Callie's cheeks as she recalled the times his hands had answered her desires without any need of words.

They made a couple of rounds inside the corral. Then Reece suggested they venture a little farther afield as he guided Moonfire into the lead along a trail that led through the oasis. They forded the stream and picked up another trail. Where the trees thinned out, a breathtaking vista of desert plain and mountains unfurled before Callie's eyes.

Reece turned in his saddle and glanced back. "We'll dismount here and walk a bit to keep your muscles loose."

They brought Moonfire and Princess to a halt and tethered the animals to the branch of a cottonwood that sheltered tufts of tall, verdant grass.

"You seem to be so at ease with horses," Callie said as they strolled along a winding path that wove in and out among the trees. "Did you ever take riding lessons?"

He laughed. "Hardly. I'd never mounted a horse in my life until I came here. Acquiring Moonfire, Princess, and Bo convinced me I needed a crash course in horse care— real fast. Carlos and his nephew taught me most everything I needed to know. The rest I learned through experience and a couple of good books on the subject."

They walked on a little farther. Where the path straggled away from the trees, they stopped to observe a patch of rain that resembled a purple bruise on the face of the cloud-shadowed mountains.

Callie allowed her gaze to dwell for a moment on Reece as he watched the rain. He stood with his feet set slightly apart, his arms crossed in a relaxed, nondefensive manner. She admired the clean, firm lines of his face, the strength inherent in his features, balanced by hints of softness at the corners of his mouth. Strange and wonderful and a little scary how her perception of him had so quickly undergone such a profound change. She viewed him now as far more gentle than hard, more tenderly compassionate than arrogant—though she conceded there was a suggestion of aloofness in the tilt of his head, the thrust of his chin.

The thought crossed her mind of waking each morning to see his face only inches from hers when she opened her eyes, of lying each night in the circle of his arms as the moon cast a silver sheen over them.

She took herself severely to task for her flight of fancy. *I can't risk the chance of falling in love with Reece Tanner.* She was grateful for the space between them. Grateful as well that any physical contact on either of their parts the past several days had been incidental rather than deliberate. If she was accurately interpreting his intent, then she could safely say that Reece held the same firm determination as she did of defusing the sparks that had been building between them.

He turned to her. "I got the feeling that night I picked you up at the market that you didn't care much for the desert. I don't suppose you've changed your mind?"

She smiled. "You're right. I didn't like the desert at first. But in a lot of ways I have changed my mind, although for a while I told myself I was crazy for letting my aunt talk me into coming here."

"Your aunt?"

"Aunt Tisha—my father's older sister. She made the reservations through her travel agent for my vacation. She's very special to me. After my mother remarried, I went to live with my aunt."

"Your aunt is your family then."

"Pretty much. I see Mom once in a while, but not often. She has her own life now." Callie hated that a hint of bitterness had crept into her voice. She'd thought she'd gotten over the horrible disappointment years ago.

"But you're still upset about the fact that your mother got married and left you behind."

"No," she countered, "I'm not the least upset."

He didn't say anything, only looked at her until she averted her gaze. Finally she was forced to acknowledge that Reece had been right. "I was sure I'd moved past that," she said in a subdued voice, "the feelings of anger, the idea that . . .'' She heard herself as if from a great distance. ''That my mother deserted me . . . and that I'd never be able to measure up to her expectations of me.''

''Maybe it was just hidden by a deeper hurt.''

''You mean what Nolan did?''

Reece took her face in his hands and made her look at him. ''Yes.''

She didn't disagree, couldn't because it was the truth. ''My mother had the habit of telling me that I was too much like my father, that if I knew what was good for me, I'd be more practical . . . like her. I guess I never realized before just how deeply I've resented her for saying that.''

''Callie, no.'' His voice was soothing, yet threaded with an underlying note of pain. ''Be true to who you are. Don't change.'' He kissed away the tears on her cheeks. ''Just let go of the resentment.''

Can I? she asked herself. The answer came as she saw sympathy and understanding in the depths of his eyes. *Yes,* she thought, *now I can.* ''Do you know,'' she said, ''that I'm here because my aunt and uncle spent their second honeymoon at Casa de la Rosa Blanca? Aunt Tisha was so enthused about the inn that she insisted I come here.''

''Second honeymoon?'' Reece stared into the distance. ''How would you feel, Callie, about spending a first honeymoon at Casa de la Rosa Blanca?'' he asked softly.

A lump filled her throat. What was he saying? Surely he couldn't be asking her to marry him.

She was both thrilled and confused at the very thought. A short while ago she'd been convinced that he was deliberately keeping her at arm's length. Now she was entertaining ideas that he was about to offer her a proposal of marriage.

The heat's frying my brain. That's the problem. ''I don't . . . That is, I think—'' *Oh, why can't I allow the dreamer in me the freedom to say yes?* Letting go wasn't going to be as easy as she'd imagined.

All at once Reece turned to her. ''Someone advised me

to try to persuade the Bennetts to advertise the inn as a sort of honeymoon hideaway. But I can see from your reaction that it was a pretty dumb suggestion.'' A nerve jumped in his cheek. ''It's time to go back. I've got work waiting for me, and your nose is in danger of getting a first-class sunburn.''

Chapter Eleven

The air always turned cool in the evenings now, and Callie began to make it a habit to visit the spa. The hot, swirling water soothed the ache in her muscles and eased the little knot of tension that seemed to form between her shoulder blades at the end of the day.

It was on one such evening that she put on her sleek turquoise bathing suit and covered it with her satin robe. After brushing out her hair, she slung a towel over her shoulder and went downstairs.

The inn dozed in candlelit quietness, causing Callie to wonder why there was no music. Then, opening the door to the outside, she heard the faint, sweet notes of the *campesino*'s guitar wafting on the night breeze.

She drew a deep breath of clean-scented air and crossed the garden to the oasis. Moonlight sifted through the branches of the trees as she made her way to the spa.

Slowing her steps, she stared into the darkness. She thought she saw something move. Realizing it was just the swaying of a tree branch stirred by the air, she walked on. The sound of Reece's chisel ringing on stone brought her to an abrupt halt.

Chink. Chink. Chink.

Callie's heart seemed to echo the steady rhythm. She hesitated, then went in the direction of the clearing where she'd secretly observed Reece before. All thought of aching muscles fled Callie's mind, and the towel slid to the ground. Her eyes widened in astonishment as she moved forward into the clearing, drawn to the half-completed statue of a man.

The carving was rough, like the first draft of one of her poems. But the guitar in the statue's hands gave away his identity, and on the stem of the guitar was a rose that looked so real she imagined that its intricately carved petals might quiver and fall off if she touched them. She reached up to feel the curve of the statue's jaw, the lips that had yet to be fully defined.

She sensed more than heard Reece's presence behind her. She turned, the satin gown swirling around her ankles with her quick movements. Time slowed, came to a stop. She watched, transfixed, as Reece approached. Moonlight gleamed off his bare shoulders.

"I was just admiring your latest work," she said.

"Were you?"

"The *campesino*," she said with a small gesture.

The music played on. It was the "Sonoran Love Song."

"You look," Reece said, "like you stepped out of a Botticelli painting." He touched her hair, winding his fingers gently around the long strands. "Chloris, from *The Birth of Venus.*"

What dream am I in now? she asked herself. "Then who are you tonight?" she said, wondering why he seemed more comfortable playing games of pretend than being himself. "Balzac? Or maybe Romeo?"

His eyes sought hers. "Is that who you want me to be, Callie? Romeo?"

No, she thought, *just be Reece Tanner*.

His gaze dropped from her face to her shoulders. "Tell me, can a statue do this?" He traced a line from her cheek to her chin with one finger. "Or this?" In the next breath he pulled her into his embrace and his lips slanted over hers.

The kiss ended, yet the "Sonoran Love Song" played on.

She pressed her face to his chest, savored the clean, musky scent of his skin.

He tipped her chin up and smiled into her eyes. " 'Love comforteth like sunshine after rain,' " he said.

"That's beautiful," she whispered. "Who—"

"Shakespeare."

"Love," she murmured. A sweet word. A bitter word. A poet's word. A word she didn't trust. She wondered why Reece had used it just now. She needed to know where he was going with this. Mustering her courage, she asked, "Have you ever been in love before?" It was the question she had wanted an answer to since her first night at Casa de la Rosa Blanca.

He tensed and dropped his arms from around her waist. He stared at the ground until the "Sonoran Love Song" came to its inevitable end. There was a moment of awkward silence. Callie noticed that the wind had grown sharper. The chill blast cut through the fabric of her robe, raising tiny bumps on her bare skin. Yet Reece seemed unfazed by the wind's bitterness.

He lifted his eyes. His features looked grim. "Yes, I was in love with someone. It was a long time ago."

With that simple confession, he had confirmed Callie's suspicions and proved Ada right in her idea that he'd had his heart broken. Hugging her arms close to her waist where his hands had so recently warmed her flesh, she waited for him to explain. She ached with the need to give him comfort with her touch, her words, as he had offered solace to her that day in the mountain meadow.

"Can you tell me about it?" she said.

He stared past her. "There isn't very much to tell. I fell in love with a woman; the relationship got serious. Then she decided she wasn't ready for that. So she moved on."

The guarded expression in his eyes warned her away from asking further questions. But she sensed there was a lot more he could tell her, if he so chose. Once, he had asked her to trust him. She had trusted him enough to reveal her deepest wounds. Why wouldn't he share his grief with her? Was it male pride? The notion that he would appear less manly in her eyes if he admitted the reasons why the relationship had failed? Surely he had no cause to doubt that she would understand.

Through the numbing silence, the wind seemed to conspire with the night to tighten its chilly fingers around her heart. She'd begun to think of the Sonoran as a place of sun and scorching heat. She'd been wrong. The desert was a place of cruel extremes. Turning from Reece, she began to walk away. The magic between them was gone. Even the *campesino* had run out of love songs to play.

"Callie—"

The raw pain in his plea drew her back. His hand reached out to caress her cheek with infinite tenderness. She shivered. Then Reece locked his arms around her waist. His mouth came down hard on hers in a wonderful kiss. The magic wasn't gone. The sparks between them had been waiting to ignite into a conflagration. Suddenly Reece broke the kiss. He held his hands rigid at his sides, his hands drawn into tight fists.

"The concert's over," he said in a husky whisper.

She sought his eyes, but he turned away, and she knew she had no choice but to face the darkness and the long walk back to the inn alone.

That night when she fell asleep it was with the taste of him scorching her lips, her heart, and his last words to her echoing in her head like a hammer blow.

She slept late the next morning. She dressed, barely aware of whether the T-shirt top she selected from the closet matched the pair of shorts she'd grabbed from a drawer. After sweeping her hair into a loose knot on top of her head, she dragged downstairs and went through the motions of eating. She put on a facade for Elena's sake, smiling and thanking her for another great meal, lest Elena start making fretful inquiries into her only guest's state of health.

In the lobby Callie hesitated, then went to the bookshelves. She scanned the spines until she discovered a hefty volume entitled *Renaissance Painters*. Running her finger down the table of contents, she found a section labeled "The Italian Renaissance" and flipped to the pages featuring the works of Botticelli.

The Birth of Venus was undeniably sensuous, hauntingly beautiful, with Chloris carried in the arms of a winged zephyr as he blew fair Venus ashore. All around the entwined pair rained roses, each engraved with a golden heart.

Below the painting were several paragraphs of text, describing how Botticelli had captured the loveliness of a spring morn, the poetic promise of bliss in the wake of winter's chill.

" 'Should we conclude from *The Birth of Venus*,' " she read aloud, " 'that we cannot gaze upon love because we are unable to bear its beauty?' "

"What do you think, Callie?"

She spun around. "Reece—" The book fell from her hands.

He snatched up the book before it crashed to the floor. "Well?" he said, placing the volume in its proper place on the shelf. "Is that what you've concluded?"

Callie stared at him and remembered the comfort of his embrace. "Yes," she said. "I think it's the only safe course. Don't you agree?"

He didn't reply as he paced over to the door that led to the courtyard. He stared out for a moment. "Ada called, said your pictures are due in today." His gaze touched on her before he opened the door. "I'll take you in to the market. We'll leave after lunch. That is, if you want."

"If that's what you want," she whispered as he slipped out the door.

* * *

"I tell ya, people just ain't reliable like they used t'be."
Ada shook her head. "That delivery man shoulda been here
an hour ago, missy." She leaned an elbow on the counter
and regarded Callie. "Tell ya what. Why don't ya go off
with Reece for a bit into town? I'm thinkin' them pictures'll
be waitin' for ya when ya get back."

Callie glanced at Reece, who was studying the label on
a package of trail mix. She wasn't at all certain that he
wanted to take her with him "for a bit into town." The
atmosphere in the van had been thick with tension on the
ride in to the market. She'd sensed several times that he
was on the verge of broaching the subject of their relationship. Instead he'd kept silent, except for a few comments
on the winter tourist season. Valiantly hiding her disappointment, she had played along.

Finally he set the package of snack mix aside and went
to pick up the box of groceries that Ada had set on the
counter. "How would you like to visit Doc Stoner?" he
said with a glance in Callie's direction.

Her heart gave a small, hopeful leap. Yet she told herself
that he was just being polite for Ada's sake. "Would you
like for me to?" she asked coolly.

He looked her in the eye. "More than anything."

Her uncertainty melted under the sudden charm of his
smile. "I'm ready to go then." She felt the touch of Ada's
hand on her arm.

"You're in for a special time," Ada said with a wink.

Evan Stoner lived, Callie discovered, in one of the little
stucco houses that were spread out in uneven rows away
from the center of Rio Puerco like crooked spokes from
the hub of a wheel. There was one cottonwood tree and a
Parry's agave decorating the barren front yard. But there
were certain homey touches too, she noticed as she accom-
panied Reece up the walk to the front door. A cobalt blue
mailbox on a white post matched the blue trim on the door

and windows. Crisp-looking curtains in a paler shade of blue hung at the two small windows flanking the door.

Reece shifted the box of groceries under one arm. He knocked once, twice. "It takes Doc a while to answer. The stroke slowed him down considerably, but with a little help from some good neighbors and friends, he's managed to keep his home and a measure of independence."

"He's not home," a voice called from behind them.

Callie looked around. A tiny woman came hurrying up to them from the house next door. She wore baggy overalls and a red kerchief around her head, and she clutched a rake in her right hand.

"Doc's cousin from Tucson came for him this morning," the woman said, squinting up at Reece, then Callie. "Doc said he was going to spend a couple of days in the city." She mopped her brow with a corner of the kerchief. "You brought his groceries out, I see."

"Sure did, Bess. Could I leave them with you?"

"Course you can." She waved the handle of the rake. "Just set the box on my porch. I'll take it inside for safe-keeping." She eyed Callie again. "Got a friend with you this afternoon, I see."

"You could say that," he said with a glance that warmed Callie through and through. "This is Callie Townsend. Callie, Bess Durham," he said by way of introduction.

"Nice to meet you," they both said at once, then laughed.

Bess Durham impressed Callie as good-hearted, one of the neighbors that Reece said took such fine care of Doc.

"I have to admit I'm a little disappointed," Callie said after she and Reece were settled in the van.

Reece started the motor. "There'll be another time."

When? she wanted to ask, thinking how quickly the days were flying by, how precious few there seemed to be left before she would have to board the plane for Milwaukee.

Instead of heading in the direction of Hawk's Market, Reece drove to the square and parked the van.

"I know you had lunch not long ago," he said, turning to her, "but would you be game for a special treat? I guarantee you won't be disappointed."

"Maybe," she said cautiously. "Not blue corn enchiladas, I hope."

"No. Something even better." He got out and came around to her side. "Come on." He gestured toward a red-and-white banner billowing above the screen door of a beige stucco building.

Callie read the sign. "Skipper's Ice Cream." She did a double take. "Skipper's?"

Reece chuckled. "Skipper John Bellow was a sea captain landlocked in the desert. As the story goes, he'd had enough of riding the high seas and was ready to fulfill his dream of a life of leisure in the Sonoran. To his way of thinking that meant opening an ice-cream parlor—and a darned successful—if unusual—one too."

A bell jangled when Reece opened the door. Callie saw what he meant by unusual. The place was a full-blown tribute to the seafaring life. Colorful fishing buoys and netting covered nearly every inch of ceiling space. Pictures of ships and a couple of rusty harpoons decorated the seafoam green walls. Each of the half dozen tables crowding the small room was adorned with a lamp fashioned in the shape of a miniature lighthouse. Behind the long, glass-fronted counter, a tall, blond-haired man was scooping ice-cream cones for a pair of teenagers. The man smiled at Callie over the pair's heads.

"I like it," she declared to Reece. "A shrine to sailors everywhere in the middle of the desert. Is that the captain?" she asked, thinking the mild-looking man hardly fit her image of a veteran of the high seas.

"No. That's the captain's son. When the captain got tired of living where there's sand but no surf, he left the business in the capable hands of his son, Jack, and set off again to ride the waves." Reece's face dipped close to hers. "I highly recommend the First Mate's Banana Split."

She read the description from a signboard above the counter. *Three scoops of ice cream—your choice—nestled on a banana raft, floating in an ocean of hot fudge, and topped with a cloud of pure whipped cream.* "Mmm. It sounds . . . sinful," she said for want of a better word. "But there's no way I could eat—"

"My thoughts were running more along the lines of sharing," Reece interjected. "Sharing a Banana Split."

"I think I can handle that," she said.

Callie couldn't remember ever eating anything so delicious before. Maybe it was because, after a few bites, Reece had taken her spoon from her hand and they had used just his spoon. Or because she could savor not only the heady blend of smooth vanilla ice cream and thick hot fudge but the virtues of being in close proximity to the man who set her pulse racing with the merest brush of his hand.

They had the place to themselves. The teenagers had wandered out, licking their cones, and Jack was apparently absorbed in decorating ice-cream cakes at a table behind the counter.

As they ate, Reece entertained her with sailor jokes— clean if slightly corny ones—and a couple of harrowing tales of shipwrecks that the captain had passed on to him.

"You have a knack for storytelling," she said.

He jabbed the spoon into the last tiny mound of melting ice cream and gooey fudge. "Yeah, a real gift."

"No, I mean it sincerely," she said, thinking that he was a great deal more modest in his assessment of himself than she had at first given him credit for.

"I know." He stared at the heaping spoon.

"And hot fudge complements your coloring very well."

He arched a brow. "What?"

She giggled and reached over to wipe away the smear of fudge that decorated his jaw.

He dropped the spoon into the dish and took her hand, pressing her fingers to his chin. "You complement me very well, Callie."

The smile froze on her lips at the implication of his words. She realized that he complemented her well too. And he made her feel alive. Her mind reeled with new possibilities—of a lifetime of wonderful kisses. A lifetime too of exploring new desert trails and mountain meadows, with Reece at her side. The tinkling of the bell over the door snapped Callie back to reality. The sight of Darla clad in tight denim cutoffs and a halter top arrested her attention.

Darla jolted to a stop, obviously surprised to see the man she called "honey" cozily sharing a dish of ice cream with his female guest from the inn. Her frigid gaze settled on Callie, then slid to Reece. As she slunk toward their table, the woman reminded Callie of a lioness on the prowl, ready to sink her claws into her hapless prey.

"Reece." His name on Darla's tongue was a throaty command.

"Hello, Darla." His greeting was noncommittal.

"Brought your guest in to do some more shopping, I see." Darla said.

To Callie's satisfaction, Reece glanced away from temptation.

Darla did a quick two-step around the table so that she was in Reece's line of vision again. "Too bad she's leaving soon. That means she'll miss out on the big dance."

Reece tossed his napkin aside and crossed his arms. "What big dance is that?"

Her smile oozed with sweetness. "Didn't you hear? Boz's brother-in-law died all of a sudden, and Boz closed up the club to fly to San Francisco for the funeral. The dance was postponed till the first Saturday of next month." She laid her hand on Reece's arm. "I'm sure you'll be available then."

"No, I'm afraid I won't, Darla."

She snatched her hand away as if he'd slapped her. Her eyes widened in shock and her face turned blotchy red.

Reece pushed his chair back. "Now if you'll excuse us, we've got some photos to pick up at the market." He didn't waste a second taking possession of Callie's arm and steering her toward the door.

Callie avoided making eye contact with Darla, but she felt the woman's hateful gaze all the way out to the sidewalk. When they were clear of Skipper's, she remarked as casually as she could manage, "Darla just reeks, with charm around you. She must love the way you dance."

Reece stared ahead, but a muscle moved in his jaw. "I thought you knew by now where I prefer to do my dancing."

Without warning he pulled her with him into a narrow side street. He wheeled her around so that she was facing him. "And I'd say it's plenty obvious who I intend to be my only partner." His hands slid slowly up from her wrists to her shoulders.

Callie looked behind her. They were in a blind alley, surrounded by stucco walls, trash cans, and a few dusty weeds growing up from the bare ground. There wasn't another soul in sight. The heat from his body rivaled that of the sun.

"I believe you know too exactly how I feel about you. But just in case you have any doubts—"

He lowered his mouth to hers, and Callie quivered in breathless anticipation of his kiss. But his lips brushed hers with only the lightest of strokes. Still, it was enough to set every nerve in her body tingling with pleasure.

"After last night," he said, his face no more than an inch from hers, "I'm pretty certain you feel the same way about me."

His eyes searched hers as if he were peering deep into her mind and reading the unspoken words that she couldn't bring herself to say. Then his mouth gently ravaged hers until she couldn't think anymore.

With a gasp she pulled away and raised her hands to his chest in an effort to put some space between them. "I . . . we hardly know each other," she protested.

"So we'll spend the rest of our lives getting to know

each other better. I've fallen in love with you, Callie. Don't you realize that?''

She closed her eyes. Before, whenever things between them had gotten intense, he'd been the first to end it. Now he showed no sign of retreating. "Reece—" She began to tremble.

Immediately Reece backed off. After a moment he took her into his arms, but protectively this time. "What is it?'' he whispered into her hair.

She clung to him as she fought for control. "I'm afraid!'' she blurted.

He cradled her chin in his hand and smoothed her cheek with his thumb. "I apologize. It was my fault for coming on too strong, for rushing you.''

"No! It isn't you." She let him see the truth in her eyes. "It's just that . . . I haven't been able to trust myself, my judgment, to get close to anyone since that happened . . . since Nolan. And sometimes I have feelings of . . . terrible anxiety.''

"I understand, Callie." He glanced away. "To be honest, I've been a little afraid too.''

His voice was soothing, his words rang with sincerity, and so she allowed herself to accept them as genuine. "I need some time, Reece. I think we both do.''

"Okay, sure," he said, staring at the ground. "I agree. We both should take time, cool off, decide where we're going. But one thing I'm sure of . . .'' He raised his eyes to hers. "I can't imagine myself living without you.''

She was on the brink of confessing that she couldn't imagine living her life without him either. Suddenly he looked toward the street.

"It seems that we've gained an audience.''

Callie turned and saw what he meant. Three young boys on bikes had stationed themselves at the alley's entrance and were gawking in their direction. Quickly she stepped back and smoothed her shirt and shorts. When she looked again, the boys were gone.

"We'd better go get your pictures," Reece said in a voice that sounded husky with longing.

Left dizzy with longing herself, all she could do was nod in mute agreement.

They walked without touching to the van and drove back to Hawk's Market, where Ada and Chico were stationed like two sentinels on either side of the entrance.

Ada grinned broadly. "Been away so long I figured you'd gone off and eloped."

Cheeks flaming, Callie forced a weak smile. She was thankful that Reece was occupied with scratching Chico behind the ears.

"Pictures are inside." Ada motioned Callie through the door. "Got a favor to ask of ya, Reece."

He stood up. "I'm always at your service, Ada."

Her mouth widened in a grin. "Flatterin' an old woman'll do ya no good, ya know. What I need from ya is to move them boxes to the cooler in back." She pointed to a pile of crates stacked near the entrance. "My arthritis's been actin' up again."

"It's as good as done." Reece hefted a crate in his hands and headed around the corner of the market, with Chico trotting along at his heels. By the time Ada joined her, Callie was fairly sure the blush was gone from her cheeks.

"Now," Ada said, leading the way to the counter, "my asking Reece to move them boxes was kinda an excuse. Mind ya, I wasn't lyin'. My arm's been hurtin' some. But what I was aimin' for was to be alone with ya for a spell. See, I got your pictures out for ya."

Callie stared in surprise. The counter was littered with her photographs. "You've looked at them all?"

"Had to make sure the delivery man didn't mess 'em up," Ada declared. "You're right good at picture-takin', missy. Them shots of Vulture's Creek brought a tear or two to my eyes. Made me think of the days when times was better for Clifford an' me, for a lot of other folks too. An' now those folks've passed on." She shook her head. "But there's a picture here that brought a tickle to my bones."

Pretty certain she already knew the answer, she asked, "Which one is that?"

"This'un here of Reece." Ada pushed the photograph into Callie's hands.

Callie's mouth went dry as she stared at the picture. Reece, in the photograph, was an object of undeniable masculine beauty. Captured for posterity were the gracefully proportioned muscles of his upper torso, the long, lean lines of his jean-clad legs, the strong, sculpted planes of his face topped by that reckless crown of black hair.

Ada chuckled. "How'd ya get him to pose for ya?"

Callie smiled lamely. "Well, I—" She glanced toward the door, expecting Reece to come charging in any second. She could see too clearly the blaze of anger darkening his features when he discovered the photo for himself.

"Doesn't matter none," Ada went on. "I never seen such a handsome man in all my seventy-five years. 'Cept for my Clifford, that is. Tell me now, missy. Are ya in love with Reece Tanner?"

Callie gingerly laid the photo on the counter, as if it threatened to burn her fingers.

"Ya are, aren't ya? I been around the barn enough times to know the signs. I'll tell ya this much, missy." Ada's voice dropped and she leaned over the counter, motioning for Callie to come closer. "There's a spark in his eyes and a spring to his step that weren't there before he knew ya. I reckon you're the best thing that's come his way in a mighty long while."

"All done, Ada."

Callie spun around to find Reece coming through the door.

He cocked his head and regarded her with amusement. "Am I missing out on something?"

Ada gave a hearty laugh. "Nothin' 't all, Reece." She scooted out from behind the counter and flapped her hands at him. ''You must have worked up a thirst movin' them boxes. Go on to the back now and fetch a soda for yourself an' one for missy here.''

Bless you. Ada, Callie thought. With one eye on Reece's retreating back, she snatched up the photos and squared the bill with Ada. By the time Reece strolled to the counter toting two bottles of pop, all the pictures were safely stowed away in Callie's purse.

''Cream soda?'' he said, and handed her one of the bottles.

His fingers stroked hers in passing, sending a warm shiver up her arm. A glance in Ada's direction showed the older woman grinning in silent approval, and Callie wished she shared Ada's simple faith in the power of love.

Chapter Twelve

Over the next two days, Callie saw Reece only from a distance. She realized that he was respecting her wishes, being as good as his word. He was allowing them both time and space to examine their feelings for each other.

At first Callie tried not to think of him, or of the decision she needed to make, afraid of what she would discover if she examined her heart too closely. Reason and wisdom told her that she shouldn't entertain—even for a minute—the idea of staying forever with him in the middle of the Sonoran Desert.

But reason and wisdom didn't take into account the desire to spend the rest of her life with the a man who had accomplished a near miracle by awakening in her a wondrous feeling of freedom and contentment.

Yet threatening to undermine her newfound happiness was a current of trepidation as dark and cold as the waters of the lake that had claimed Nolan's life. It whispered that her happiness could turn on a twist of fate into bitterness and sorrow, and that, if it did, the wounds were apt to prove fatal.

So she determined that for the moment it was in her best interest to distract herself. She wanted desperately to rekindle her initial enthusiasm for compiling a dazzling portfolio of photographs that would knock the wire-rimmed glasses off Gunther Graham's proper patrician nose and pave the way for an invitation to exhibit her work in his next show. First on her agenda was to spend most of her time the next day or so exploring Vulture's Creek at greater length.

After scrutinizing her developed photos, she'd found them to be a mixed bag. Several of them—the picture of Marcos, the stills of the livery and the barbershop, a few that she'd shot in the meadow—were very good, at least as far as her subjective eye could discern. And the photograph of Reece was nothing short of spectacular. But the rest were average at best, and of the fifty or so shots, she estimated that only a handful would be apt to gain even a passing nod of approval from Gunther.

She hadn't known quite what to do with the picture of Reece. Every time she looked at it, her heart fluttered as if it had sprouted wings and wanted to escape her chest, and her fingers fairly burned as they slid over the image of his manly physique and handsome features. All of her good intentions threatened to derail faster than a freight train running at full throttle toward a flaming bridge. With a sigh, she tucked the photo under her folded slips in the bureau drawer, where it would safely lie until she weakened and took it out again.

Elena was her usual cheerful self as she served Callie breakfast.

"You look rested. You must have slept well," the housekeeper remarked.

Callie smiled over the rim of her coffee cup but didn't confess that the few hours she'd been able to sleep had been filled with weird and wonderful dreams of Reece and of being held in his arms under the full moon while around them the statues waltzed in solemn precision.

Elena didn't bat an eye when Callie asked for a canteen of water and a piece of fruit and sandwich "to eat later." She felt a bit guilty telling the housekeeper that she planned on spending some time in the oasis, though it wasn't a bold-faced lie, since she'd be traveling through the oasis on her way to Vulture's Creek. She'd decided that the best

course for her was to adopt a "less said the better" attitude
and not volunteer information.

"Have a good time," Elena called as Callie left the dining room with the canteen of water and a substantial lunch
stuffed in her knapsack.

A film of clouds muddied the clarity of the western horizon, and there was a whisper of coolness to the air stirring
the leaves. When she came to the corral, Callie debated
whether to saddle up Princess rather than walk to Vulture's
Creek. She looked for Reece, but he wasn't at the barn.
What if he came later and noticed the mare was missing?
Would he assume that his guest had taken off for the ghost
town against his advice?

What does it matter? she asked herself.

The mare trotted to the fence. Callie greeted her with a
soft "Hello, girl," and a pat on the nose. Reluctantly she
decided to go on alone and not risk raising Reece's suspicions. "Another time," she told Princess.

The first place Callie headed when she reached Vulture's
Creek was the Silver Lode hotel. With a rush of anticipation she peered through the gaping hole that had once been
the front door. Her hopes for a good photo shoot quickly
dimmed. The inside of the old lodging was a gutted-out
ruin. Not a stick of furniture was to be seen in the dreary,
cavelike room of what was once the lobby. The wide, curv-
ing stairwell in the center of the room dared Callie to try
her luck at negotiating its rickety steps. Callie peered up-
ward into darkness. She shuddered to think what she might
find if she were foolish enough to risk climbing the stairs.

Sunlight streaming through the gaping windows on either
side of the front door cast the stairwell in a hazy amber
glow. Cobwebs hung like ragged, gilded doilies from what
remained of the banister, and a single rusted metal stool
stood in the shadows behind the stairwell. Callie took a
couple of shots of the stairs, then checked out the rest of
the lobby. The silence seemed to magnify the sound of her

boots beating a rhythm against the buckled wooden floor, the lazy drone of a fly overhead.

To her disappointment all she found of interest were fragments of colored glass and a few broken shards of pottery. She bent to examine one of the shards and ran her fingers along the delicate scroll design still visible on the piece. She started to stow the shard in her knapsack, then thought better of it.

"Let sleeping ghosts lie," she murmured, returning the fragment to the spot where she'd found it. A rush of dizziness caused her to nearly lose her balance as she got to her feet. Maybe the heavy odor of dust and decay was making her woozy. Or maybe she needed a drink of water. She unscrewed the cap on the canteen and took several swallows. She'd seen enough of the Silver Lode for one day.

A rustling sound from behind her brought her to a stop. She cast a nervous glance over her shoulder.

Suddenly a horrific screech, like the scolding tongue of a banshee, reverberated off the walls. Callie swung around just in time to see an owl swooping down from the darkness at the top of the stairwell. It dove past her with another screech and, with a great flapping of its speckled wings, flew out one of the windows.

Heart pounding in her chest, Callie made her way on shaky legs to the door. She gazed up and spied the spotted owl perched on a post mere yards from her head. It blinked its huge eyes and stared at her as if to scold, "You scared me half to death too, you know!"

Slowly, so as not to frighten him away, Callie lifted her camera and took his picture. Capturing the handsome bird on film might prove to be her best photo opportunity of the day.

Delving into the knapsack, she fished out a sandwich and ate it, with the owl still observing her in stately silence. Then she set off for the grove of trees behind the hotel. She found the cemetery and paused to look at the tombstones. Most of them were crumbling to dust, and all of the inscriptions were illegible except for the grave of the man who had died in the mine. The stone bore a simple ivy border and read: *Unknown male, approx. age forty-five years. May God rest his soul.*

Callie snapped a couple of pictures of the stone. Looking around, she caught sight of what appeared to be a wall partly hidden by vines and branches. She made her way through the brush and discovered a remarkably well pre-served cabin whose windows and doors were boarded up.

As she approached, she recalled her odd dream of the statues coming to life and leading her through the thicket. They'd pointed at something; then she'd seen the shadow of a man. The dream had disturbed her, although she didn't believe in portents. Yet it occurred to her now that if she hadn't ventured into the thicket, she would never have known of the cabin's existence.

She tested one of the rough slats crisscrossing the door. The nails holding the slat in place loosened from their moorings in the wood; another hard tug and the slat fell away. The other slats gave way with equal ease.

The door opened with a creak, and Callie stared into the murky interior of the cabin. The place was furnished, or partially so, with a leaning table and two chairs with their seats missing. A bureau without drawers stood against one wall, and a row of cupboards hugged the opposite wall. A doorway led off on either side of the main room. A stone hearth occupied one corner. Dust filmed the floor of the hearth; the chimney was blackened with soot.

Callie had that same eerie sense of trespassing where she didn't belong. She wondered if the vagrant had stayed in the cabin for a time. The place would have given him a reasonable amount of shelter, and a fire banked in the hearth would provide warmth when the temperature dipped lower at night.

She peeked through one of the doorways. Thin fingers of sunlight illuminated the metal frame of a bedstead.

Did Reece know about the cabin? Perhaps he'd been the one who had secured the windows and doors, just as he'd boarded over the opening of the mine after he'd found the vagrant's body. He might have even led the sheriff from Nogales to the cabin on a search for clues as to who the dead man was or where he'd come from.

Callie discovered that the other room was empty except for a dirt-encrusted basin and a cracked mirror propped up against a wall. She crossed to the cupboards. Fearful that a tarantula or scorpion might be lurking behind the doors, she hesitated a fraction of a second before peering inside.

There were no scary critters, but there were a couple of tin plates, a cup, a few pieces of cutlery, and several ancient-looking tin cans minus their labels.

She took a close-up shot of the open cupboards where the sunlight reflected off the plates and cup. After adjusting the aperture on the Nikon, she framed the hearth in the lens and snapped a picture of it. As she bent to inspect the fireplace, she made a startling discovery. A portion of the stone slid away beneath her hand, revealing a space between the hearth and the wall. She peered into the opening. Bits of paper littered the floor. Deftly she poked her hand into the space and pulled out several of the scraps. The paper was yellowed with age, but by holding the shreds up to the light, she saw that once there'd been writing on them. A few blurred letters were visible, and one complete word. It was a word that had seemed to shadow her every move from almost the moment of her arrival in the Sonoran Desert.

''Love,'' she murmured, tracing the letters with her finger.

She set the tattered paper aside and peered into the space again. There was something farther back, nestled against the wall. Reaching in, Callie drew out an oblong metal box. The box was secured with a small rusted padlock. She shook the box and felt the contents shift back and forth. She guessed there was a bundle of papers inside.

Maybe it's a map that'll lead me to buried treasure, she thought with a smile. Or would the contents reveal clues as to the identity of the vagrant?

She tried the lock. It wouldn't give, but it looked fragile enough to yield to a good blow from a hammer—if only she had one. She glanced around for something that might substitute for a hammer, and remembered the boards she'd torn off the door to gain entrance to the cabin.

A sudden loud crack of thunder set the walls and floors trembling. Callie dropped the box and scrambled to her feet to look out at the sky. Though the sun was shining overhead, dark clouds were advancing like stealthy warriors over the crest of the hills. She chided herself for not paying more attention to the weather. If she didn't hustle, she'd be in for a drenching—and worse if she didn't make it across the arroyo while the gully was dry.

She shoved the box into the hole between the hearth and the wall and pushed the stone into place. Since she had no means of nailing the boards over the door, she settled for pulling the door shut and heaping the boards in a pile beside it.

She passed through the arroyo safely and was close to the corral when the first drops of rain began to hit the ground. Her attention was arrested by the sight of Reece and Marcos standing beside Bo at the far end of the corral. Reece had his arm around the boy's shoulder, and the pair appeared to be oblivious to the impending downpour. Callie was oblivious too as she watched Reece tousle Marcos's hair. The boy's happy laughter was carried to her on the rising wind.

As if he'd known she was standing there, observing, Reece turned his head and smiled. He took a step in her direction, hesitated, then made an abrupt turn and walked toward the barn. But Marcos waved excitedly and came running up to her.

The boy's eyes shone like tiny, luminous saucers against his brown skin.

"Hi!" he said.

Callie smiled. "Hi."

He danced around her as if he couldn't contain himself. "Guess what?"

"What, Marcos?"

"Mr. Tanner said Mr. Bennett told him he could buy a colt this winter and—"

A boom of thunder interrupted him. Callie winced.

Marcos eyed her curiously. "You scared of thunder?"

"No," she said, telling a half-truth, "but I don't exactly relish getting drenched. Go ahead. What were you about to say?"

"Mr. Tanner's gonna get the colt, and he said if I take good care of Bo an' always remember to groom him, then when I'm thirteen he might be able to persuade Mr. Bennett to let me have Bo as my very own horse!"

"That's wonderful, Marcos. It sounds like you're getting a good start on those hundred horses you told me you wanted to own someday."

He cast her a shy grin. "Yeah, I guess so." Marcos looked at the sky. "Uh-oh! You'd better run or you're gonna get wet."

A volley of raindrops pelted Callie's head. She grinned and gave the boy's shoulder a quick squeeze. "I think you're right, Marcos." With a hasty "See you later," she dashed back to the inn. The floodgates of heaven gave way just as she ducked into the lobby.

Callie ate her dinner to the sound of raindrops dashing against the windows. Afterward she curled up in a chair in the lobby and tried to absorb herself in a mystery that she'd dislodged from one of the bookshelves. Around her the candles sputtered and hissed in the sconces, while outside the storm continued its violent show. She tried her best to focus on the story, but between the booms of thunder and the intermittent flickering of the lamps that made her wonder if a blackout was imminent, she finally gave up and laid the book on her lap.

Her mind turned to the surprise discovery she'd made in the abandoned cabin. She wished she felt free to confide in Reece, to ask his advice as to what he thought should be done with the padlocked metal box whose contents might solve the mystery of the dead man's identity.

Despite the inclement weather, she suddenly longed for Reece to appear at the door that led in from the courtyard. She could see him standing on the threshold, dripping water, his T-shirt sculpted to the sleek muscles of his chest, his hair wet and glistening in the candlelight. Their eyes would meet, and he'd say, *"I needed to see you tonight. I thought you might be a little lonely and—well, I'm kind of lonely too."*

From the corner of her eye she saw Elena bustling into the lobby.

A frown pleated the housekeeper's brow. "I just remembered, Miss Townsend, that I'd forgotten to light a fire in the hearth. The air is very chilly tonight, don't you think?"

"Yes, now that you mention it." Callie put the book aside. For the first time she noticed that her hands felt cold, her fingertips numb.

Elena talked as she stacked pieces of wood in the fireplace. "It's been many years since I've seen it rain like this at night so late in the year. It isn't a good sign, I'm afraid."

"What do you mean?"

"It's only superstition, Miss Townsend, but there is a local saying that if an autumn rain falls past midnight over one's roof, then someone in the household will have reason to shed many tears before two moons have passed." The housekeeper struck a long match and held it to a rolled-up piece of paper. "It was after such a storm that tragedy came to visit this house."

A cold tremor crawled up Callie's back as she watched Elena toss the paper torch onto the logs. "You mean the night that Mallory mistook his daughter for the *campesino*.''

''Yes.'' Elena lifted a poker from a stand beside the hearth and bent to rearrange the pile of wood. Sparks showered and leaped up the chimney as one of the logs caught fire. ''I'm sorry.'' She looked over her shoulder. ''You're our guest and it's our desire that your stay be a refreshing one. There is no need for you to be concerned about tales and superstitions that are invented by idle old people with nothing better to do. Anyway, you don't believe such gossip, do you?''

Callie summoned a smile, but she noticed that she'd curled her hands into fists in her lap. ''No, of course I don't,'' she said.

''Good. Now how about some Mexican chocolate?''

''Mexican chocolate?''

Elena gave a gentle laugh. ''That's hot cocoa with a dash of cinnamon added for spice. It is very tasty. Let me get you a cup.''

The housekeeper returned with a small tray that held the steaming chocolate, which was topped by a swirl of whipped cream.

Callie stared into the fire and sipped the sweet beverage. But even the hot, spicy chocolate and the heat from the burning logs failed to warm her, and when she'd finished the last of the cocoa, she went upstairs to bed. The screeching sound of the wind through the courtyard reminded her of the cry of the owl that had swooped down from the rafters at the Silver Lode. But the drumbeat of raindrops against the windows was the last thing she heard before she fell asleep.

Callie woke with sudden alertness. Pushing the covers aside, she sat up and swung her legs over the bed. The storm was over; a perfect three-quarter moon was framed in a pane of glass. She held her arm up to the light so that she could read the face of her watch. It was just past three

A.M. She wondered if the rain had stopped before midnight. She knew she had dreamed of the *campesino*, or at least of his shadowy presence. He'd been playing the "Sonoran Love Song" while a storm raged over the desert, and she'd been crying without knowing why.

Callie brought her hands to her face. Her cheeks were moist with tears. If she'd only been dreaming, then why was she crying, and how could she still be hearing the music?

She got out of bed and padded over to the window. The sound of the "Sonoran Love Song" filled the night air. In the courtyard below the statues stood frozen in ghostly splendor as if they too were mesmerized by the music. Callie slipped into her robe and went downstairs. The candles were all extinguished, but a few embers glowed red among the ashes in the hearth and the smell of wood smoke hung in the air.

Callie pushed on the door that led into the courtyard and discovered that it was unlocked. Anticipation sent a quiver along her nerves. The tangy odor of greasewood mingled with the bracing smell of clean air. Pools of moonlit rainwater were strung across the yard like silver beads in a dark chain. Lured on by the sultry strains of the "Love Song," Callie moved past the statues, barely aware of the frosty breeze that nipped at her legs.

She glimpsed the outline of a man merging with the statue of Balzac, and her pulse did a wild dance in her throat. Could it be Reece, waiting to whisper an eager invitation to waltz with him under the starry desert sky? Or was she within a heartbeat of uncovering the identity of the *campesino?*

She was doomed to disappointment. What she'd believed was a man's form was actually the shadow of another sculpture cast by the moon. Stubbornly she pressed on, even though she was beginning to suspect that she was pursuing a phantom.

The leafy branches of the cottonwoods nearly eclipsed

the moon as Callie entered the oasis. The music seemed to
come from everywhere at once—like the sound of Reece's
hammer and chisel striking stone. For a moment Callie felt
disoriented. Then she relied on her instincts to guide her,
and they were telling her to head for the clearing.

The statue of the *campesino* was bathed in a milky glow.
As Callie approached, her eyes glimpsed the flash of silver
guitar strings in the moonlight and she came to an abrupt
stop on a sharp intake of breath.

Are my eyes deceiving me again? she wondered.

Though he was half-hidden behind the statue, Callie saw
enough of the peasant to know that he wasn't a phantom
or the shadow of a renegade cloud. His slight build and
gently sloping shoulders indicated that he was the same
man she'd glimpsed in the courtyard the night she'd been
rudely awakened by the Peloskies' argument.

"I don't mean to intrude," she said, "but your music is
so lovely. I've heard a great deal about you, that you're the
campesino. I just had to find out—"

"*Sí,* but of course," he replied in a heavy Hispanic ac-
cent. "I would have been disappointed if you had not found
me."

"You would?"

He laughed softly. "You shouldn't be surprised. I saw
the sadness in your eyes the night you arrived. That's why
I've been playing my music for you, *señorita.*"

"Please call me Callie."

"Callie. *Sí.* Were you aware that your name means
'beautiful blossom'? I'm being truthful when I say it is a
fitting name for you."

The *campesino* stepped out from behind the statue, and
Callie got her first good look at him. Though his face was
lined and weathered, his hair shone dark and thick with
only a few streaks of white visible in the moonlight. There
was a hint of vulnerability in the set of his mouth, and his
features possessed warmth and charm.

I don't wonder that Laurel fell in love with you, she

thought. "I know about Laurel," she said, "and that you play your music for her too."

"Ah . . . Laurel." His tongue caressed the name. " 'The victor's crown.' " He propped the guitar against the statue. "A bitter irony, isn't it, to be given such a name? Who told you about the 'Love Song'?"

The twinkle in his eyes hinted that he already knew the answer. "It's the same man who's immortalizing you in stone."

He chuckled. "Reece. *Sí.* The 'ardent one.' "

"You seem to know a lot about names and their meanings."

"I've made a search of many things," he replied. "When a man has much time on his hands to contemplate the past, his sorrow soon turns into . . . *desesperación.*" His face twisted in an expression of pain. "A man's heart—his mind—is consumed by his hatred for the one who caused him such terrible sadness. He fears—no, begs—that . . . he wants to die."

The older man turned to the statue and stroked the petals of the granite rose. "The fortunate man," he went on in a hushed voice, "is the one who seeks some . . . work, an activity that will become his passion. Then—*muy bien!*—if God looks on him with mercy, balance is restored to his heart and his mind."

Is he talking about Reece as much as about himself? He could be talking about me as well. She was starting to think too that the *campesino*'s identity wasn't as much of a mystery as she'd once believed.

"I've gotten acquainted with a charming young boy who lives nearby," she said. "His name is Marcos, and we've become fast friends. I can tell that he really loves his grandfather because he speaks very highly of him."

His features softened. "Marcos. 'The little warrior.' Sometimes it seems that a name doesn't suit the person. But then . . . someday it might prove to be so." He sighed. "Marcos believes that he has a grandfather. But the man he speaks highly of is, in fact, a more distant relative who had no children of his own because he never found the strength to love anyone but his Laurel. His heart is like *la brújula*—that is, the compass—that holds one course. But he was greatly blessed by the kindness of a niece who took him into her home and made him feel welcome as part of her large and happy family.''

Callie saw the elderly man through tear-misted eyes. A smile illumined his gaze. ''I'm glad, Carlos,'' she said. ''I know a little of how you feel. I lived with my aunt for many years, and she still frets over me as if I were a teenager.''

''*Sí,* of course. It is because she cares for you. There's someone else who cares for you too, Callie—a man who has found within himself the strength to love again.''

Callie couldn't bear to look at him, though she longed to ask him how he knew that Reece loved her. Had Reece told him as much? Or had he seen them locked in a passionate embrace under the stars? She made a pretext of consulting her watch and was shocked to see how much time had slipped by while they were talking.

''I shouldn't have kept you.'' She touched his arm. ''It's very chilly, and I'm afraid you might—''

''No, *por favor.* You mustn't apologize. You have brought me much joy tonight.''

''Could you tell me one more thing, Carlos?''

''Perhaps.''

''What does your name mean?''

He shook his head. '' 'The strong man.' ''

Callie smiled. ''I would say yours is the most appropriate name of all.''

''Ah, you please an old man by your words, Callie. Now before you leave me . . .'' He reached behind the statue.

Callie gasped at what she saw. His countenance glowed with the bright radiance of an angel's as he held out to her a perfect long-stemmed white rose.

''Go then,'' he said, ''and may you dream of the one who cares for you.''

Chapter Thirteen

Callie woke refreshed, though she'd slept only a few hours. The first thing she saw when she opened her eyes was the white rose nestled beside her pillow, sunlight streaming over its delicate petals. She pressed her face to the bloom and drew in its softly sweet scent. A feeling of gentle lassitude enfolded her. She smiled, knowing that her conversation with the *campesino* had been as real as the perfectly formed rose that he had given her.

She remembered falling asleep when the first fringe of dawn was brushing warm streaks of crimson and gold across the dark Sonoran sky. She remembered too that she had dreamed, and as she sat up in bed, fully awake, she recalled the dream with striking clarity.

It had been January, the anniversary of Nolan's burial, and she'd gone to visit his grave. Snow piled in drifts around the tombstones, and the whole earth had been reduced to a wintry landscape of white and gray. Icy needles of wind pricked her cheeks as she'd stood staring at the whitened mound of earth. She'd expected to cry, but no tears came. She'd expected the familiar burst of anger to rage through her like a forest fire out of control. But there'd been no hot surge of anger. Nor had there been the usual heavy burden of guilt and sadness, or even a hint of fear. The old terrors were gone, and she'd known then that the nightmares about Nolan were over. She'd raised her eyes to see the sun breaking through the clouds. And wondrously, as if by a miracle, Reece had appeared at her side. With complete trust she'd taken hold of his outstretched hand, not once looking back as they walked toward the light of a lustrous new day.

"And I'm not going to look back," she vowed to herself, "not ever again."

She bounded out of bed, showered in record time, and dressed in fresh jeans and an aqua blue knit top. She slathered sunblock on her arms and face, dusted her cheeks with blusher to highlight their natural color, and glossed her lips with pale pink lipstick. She began to twist her hair into a plait, then changed her mind and merely brushed out the tangles, letting her hair tumble freely over her shoulders. On her way out she grabbed her hat, her camera, and a few extra rolls of film, optimistic that she could persuade Reece to let her take his picture sitting astride Moonfire. In fact, she felt giddily optimistic at the moment that she could persuade him to do most anything she wanted him to.

"You look . . . ." Elena paused in her routine of pouring Callie a cup of coffee. "Glowing," she said at last. "Off somewhere again today, are you?"

"I'm not sure of my plans yet." The only thing she was certain of was her love for Reece, and her determination to tell him so at the earliest possible opportunity.

Elena set a platter of French toast and sausage on the table. "Well . . . ." She smiled broadly. "I believe that Mr. Tanner has gone to the stable barn, if you want to see him."

Callie ate quickly, hardly tasting her food. Elena returned to ask if her guest would like a filled canteen to take with her that morning. Callie started to say no, then changed her mind. The day seemed to suddenly burgeon with shining possibilities and plausible reasons for toting along a canteen of cold water. Maybe Reece would suggest they take Moonfire and Princess out on the trails. Or that the two of them go for a leisurely—and romantic—stroll through the oasis. Or why shouldn't she entertain the hope that he would acquiesce and accompany her to Vulture's Creek?

As she walked toward the corral, other possibilities presented themselves in her mind. Like the last pieces of a puzzle finally falling into place, she saw her future clearly. With no regrets, she would give notice at the law firm, leave the hectic pace of city life behind. She might miss the chance to one day have her photographs on display at Gunther Graham's gallery, but she was certain in her heart that there would be other chances at other galleries. She remembered how, that afternoon in the meadow, Reece had encouraged her to pursue her dream. Someday she and Reece might even be invited to participate in a husband-and-wife show—his sculptures and her photographs.

Her one regret would be living so far away from her aunt. But that didn't seem like such a drawback when she considered her aunt's warm memories of Casa de la Rosa Blanca. She doubted it would take much coaxing to persuade Aunt Tisha to visit often. She could see her aunt's eyes light with approval on meeting Reece. She was just as confident that he'd be equally fond of Tisha. He'd even expressed a desire to visit the Apostle Islands someday. The thought of being the one to show him the islands sent a ripple of excitement through her.

Her pace quickened. Approaching the corral, she saw no sign of Reece, so she headed on to the barn. She called out his name. There was no answer. Inside the barn, Princess and Bo were in their stalls. But Moonfire's stall stood empty.

Callie sat down on a hay bale near Princess's stall. The mare stuck her nose through the slats to nuzzle Callie's palm.

"Hello, pretty girl. You wouldn't happen to know where Moonfire and his master are off to, would you?" The mare snorted softly. "I didn't think so. I guess I'll have to be patient again, won't I?"

As the minutes crept by, Callie's restlessness grew. *Why*

not do something useful? she reasoned. She thought of the padlocked box in the cabin at Vulture's Creek. After some searching, she located a small hammer among the assortment of tack and tools hung on pegs along the wall of the barn. After a couple of failed attempts, she managed to saddle Princess as Reece had taught her. By riding to the ghost town instead of walking, she'd save a fair amount of time and be back at the corral by early afternoon. Maybe Reece would be there, waiting for her.

Callie's initial nervousness on guiding the mare out of the barn eased as Princess settled into a comfortable pace on the trail. When she came to the slope that led down into the arroyo, Callie saw that a narrow stream of water trickled through the center of the gully. Even now, despite a dazzling display of sunshine and blue sky, clouds hugged the tops of the hills above Vulture's Creek.

Callie dismounted and tethered the mare to a post in the shade of a sycamore. She walked on alone, toting the hammer, the canteen, and her camera. She found the cabin in the same state as she'd left it—the gaping entrance, the boards stacked by the door, and the quiet, like an eerie, invisible presence pervading everything.

She didn't stop to take any pictures but went on inside and crossed over to the hearth. Sliding the loose stone away, she pulled out the box and sat down on the floor.

She hesitated, turning the box over in her hands. *Should I really do this?* she wondered. But if she didn't open the box, who would? For that matter, what were the chances that someone else would discover the cabin? Marcos had told her that he sometimes took a shortcut through the ghost town. But Vulture's Creek was definitely off the beaten track, and Reece had made it clear that he didn't conduct tours to the town.

After several hard blows from the hammer, the lock broke apart. Callie cracked the lid open and turned the box upside down. A large brown envelope fell out, along with a sheaf of papers, bound with a piece of yellowed parch-

ment and held together by two rubber bands. She reached
for the envelope first and shook the contents into her lap.

Photos tumbled out, a dozen or so altogether, faded
somewhat by age. Callie began to thumb through them. All
of them were of the same couple—a dark-haired man with
a neatly trimmed beard and a petite woman with curly au-
burn hair. Behind the couple, clusters of balloons framed a
large banner with the word *Congratulations* written on it.
The couple was dressed casually, the man in black slacks
and a red crew top, the woman in a patterned sundress. In
one of the photos she was feeding him a piece of cake; in
another they were kissing. Yet a third showed them holding
a framed piece of paper between them.

These are pictures of a wedding! Callie thought. Was
she looking at the man whose body Reece had found? She
flipped the pictures over; there was writing on the back of
them. Moving to a spot where there was more light, she
held one of the pictures up to the sun. Details sprang to
her attention that she hadn't noticed before. The wedding
band on the man's left hand. A dimple in the woman's right
cheek. And something far more astonishing.

Callie went rigid, unable at first to believe what her eyes
were telling her. The man was no stranger to her. It was
Reece! Never mind the beard and long hair. Never mind
that he was perhaps ten years older now and a good ten to
fifteen pounds leaner than he appeared in the pictures. She
recognized the beloved features, the indomitable eyes.
Half-dazed, she turned over the photo of the pair holding
the framed piece of paper.

" 'Ken,' " she read under her breath. She went on, just
able to make out the words. " 'Ken is now officially Dr.
Kenton Rhodes. And he has the credentials to prove it!' "

Callie sat for a moment in quiet shock, unable to com-
prehend anything beyond the obvious fact that Reece was
not Reece Tanner but a man named Kenton Rhodes. And
Kenton Rhodes was a physician. *Had been* a physician, she
corrected herself. She recalled asking him in a teasing way

if he was a doctor. His expression had darkened. Then he'd given her a spiel about being a jack-of-all-trades and declared that he'd just as soon leave the practice of medicine to people like Doc Stoner.

"Why?" Her voice echoed in the silence as Elena's sober warning came back to haunt her.

"If an autumn rain falls past midnight over one's roof, then someone in the household will have reason to shed many tears before two moons have passed."

Elena had tried to dismiss the superstition as idle gossip. Maybe she shouldn't have.

With shaking hands, Callie forced herself to turn over each picture and read the scribbled message on the back. Incredible how much she was able to learn about him in a few short sentences. His wife's name was Anna Beth. The cake was red velvet—his favorite. He'd been awarded his license to practice medicine one week before the surprise party in his honor. His residency had been in internal medicine with a special interest in orthopedics.

No wonder he knew so much about heel spurs and the treatment of blisters! Questions crowded her mind. So many questions. Where was his wife? Had she died? Were they divorced? Did they have children? Where had they lived?

He'd revealed he'd had a "relationship" with a woman in the past. He'd said nothing about being married.

Callie no longer believed that he was from Seattle. How could she believe anything he'd told her about himself? But what could possibly have happened to cause him to abandon his profession, and perhaps his wife as well, to change his name and become the manager of an out-of-the-way hotel in the Sonoran Desert?

How ironic it seemed to her now that she'd considered Nolan to be the worst kind of jerk when it appeared Reece was cut from the same cloth! How had he managed to deceive so many people? Even Ada and the *campesino*, with their age and wisdom, hadn't a clue about him. They believed that all he needed was for someone to love him. Callie was appalled to think that someone was her.

Yet, in spite of her anger and confusion, she couldn't quite convince herself that Reece had purposely misled her. The pain in his eyes when he'd told her he'd once been in love was real. And she couldn't shake the idea that his preoccupation with chiseling couples out of stone was fueled by some inner conflict that he hadn't yet come to terms with. What caused that conflict, though, was more of a mystery to her than ever. If Reece truly loved her, how could he not have trusted her enough to know that she would accept the truth about his past—no matter what the truth might be?

Not Reece, she reminded herself. *Kenton. Kenton Rhodes.* She tried it out on her tongue, attempted to match the name to the man she knew. Or thought she knew. "Kenton Rhodes" didn't fit, she decided. "Reece Tanner" did.

Callie laughed out loud; the laugh ended in a sob. She sat staring at the pictures, unable to move. She lost track of time. Glancing up, she was shocked to see that the sky had darkened; the sun was gone. As if she were acting out the final scene of a nightmare, she picked up the sheaf of papers. Would she find an explanation there as to why the man she'd heedlessly fallen in love with was not who he claimed to be?

Her fingers fumbled with the rubber bands. One of the bands broke and snapped against her wrist, burning her skin. She lifted the first folded sheet from the bundle. The page was covered with writing—Anna Beth's? It was a letter.

There was no salutation, just *How could you!* flung across the top of the page. Callie's gaze dropped to the next crookedly written lines.

How could you do this to us—to me—to my family? How could you throw it all away, Ken? How could

*you betray me, our future, everything we've dreamed
about and hoped for? How could you do this and say
that you love me?*

With both fascination and horror, Callie realized that the
angry accusations, the gut-wrenching questions, were a perfect reflection of all that she had ever wanted to say to
Nolan Jamison—if only she'd been given the chance.

Callie's stomach clenched in a painful knot. She couldn't
bear to read any more. What Reece—Ken—had done to
hurt his wife so badly seemed irrelevant now. She had been
in Anna Beth's shoes; she knew how the wounds of betrayal festered, how bitterly long they lingered.

Raising tear-filmed eyes, Callie saw lightning flash
through a gap in one of the windows.

It's going to storm, she thought with a feeling of de-
tachment, as though the lightning and thunder were make-
believe instead of real.

She looked at the sheaf of papers. Morbid curiosity and
a loud clap of thunder drove her to make a decision. She
would take the papers with her, secrete them into her room,
examine them that night. Whatever else she learned about
Reece, she knew in her heart that she couldn't spend another day under the same roof with him.

She made up her mind. She would call the airport in
Tucson first thing in the morning, request that a limousine
be dispatched immediately to the inn. She would devise an
excuse, tell Elena that her aunt was home from France and
had taken ill, or that her employer needed her to return at
once. She would go before Reece got wind of her plans.

She hastily gathered the photos together and returned
them to the box. Then she rose, the box tucked under one
arm, the sheaf of papers clutched in her hand.

Thunder shook the cabin walls again. In the quiet that
followed, she heard a footstep on the floor, the sound of
her name. Her heart gave a slam in her chest. She stopped
and spun around.

Reece stood in the doorway. His face mirrored the threat of the approaching storm as he advanced on her. His gaze fell on the metal box, and Callie felt the full force of his fury. Yet she couldn't move.

He covered the distance between them in a few swift strides. He locked his fingers over her arms, and the box went crashing against the hearth. The papers fell out of her hands. She watched the sheets spiral to the floor like a flock of wounded doves as Reece backed her into a corner. Then he grasped hold of her chin and made her look at him.

"What," he demanded, "do you think you're doing here?"

Chapter Fourteen

Callie opened her mouth to respond but no words came out. A battle raged inside of her as her gaze warred with Reece's, a milieu of conflicting feelings that refused to fall into any sort of logical pattern. Reece both excited her and frightened her. His nearness brought her exquisite delight while her heart was crumbling into a thousand pieces. One instant she believed that if he would only kiss her, then she would know that whatever happened to cause Anna Beth to accuse him of betrayal, he was not at fault and that she could forgive him. The next, she prayed that he would never touch her again.

Illogically, she'd never been more sure that she loved him. Yet her sense of anger and confusion was so great that she had to fight the urge to slap his face.

His fingers tightened around her arms, and she winced, though he was not actually hurting her.

"Why did you come here, Callie?"

On searching his eyes, she knew that he wasn't just mad. She saw a kaleidoscope of emotions as confusing as her own. Fear. Regret. Sadness. Uncertainty. Love.

"Why did you lie to me?" she challenged, her voice trembling with hurt.

His jaw clenched. "I never lied to you!"

His sharp words echoed like thunder through the cabin, and something in Callie snapped. With a quick move, she

173

wrenched free from his grasp. She spotted the letter from Anna Beth beside his foot and made a lunge for it. "Never lied?" She waved the letter in front of him. "*Dr.* Kenton Rhodes!"

He visibly paled. Snatching the letter out of her hand, he paced the length of the room and back. In the silence Callie heard raindrops nailing the cabin's roof, her heart mimicking the drumbeat sound. Finally he stopped in front of her. A look of sorrow filled his eyes.

"There is no Dr. Kenton Rhodes," he said.

She could only stare at him, incredulous. "How can you tell me that? I saw the pictures of you and—" She couldn't bring herself to say the name Anna Beth aloud.

His shoulders slumped. "It's true, Callie," he said very quietly. "It's true."

Is he insane? she thought. *Or am I?*

He looked at the papers scattered over the floor. "Is the letter all you read?"

"Yes."

He regarded her for a moment as if he doubted her truthfulness. Then he threw the letter down and strode to the window. "We have to get out of here," he said. "Now!" He turned on his heel. "You have no idea of the danger we're in, do you?"

Danger? she wanted to scream. *I know all about the dangers of getting involved with a man like you!* She got away just as he reached for her.

She ran, wanting only to escape the panic and the darkness that threatened to engulf her. She searched for the graveyard through the driving rain. It wasn't where she was sure it should be. Frantically she realized she'd made a wrong turn. She heard Reece calling her name, but she refused to look back as she plunged on in an attempt to find her way out of the thicket.

A streak of lightning sped like a comet from the sky to the ground, followed by a blast of thunder. A metallic odor hung in the air.

Callie gave a startled cry and changed direction again. Her lungs ached with the sheer effort of breathing. Her rain-soaked clothes clung to her body, chilling her skin. The wind whipped her sodden hair across her eyes, blocking her vision. Finally she spotted a break in the trees and staggered toward it.

"Callie, no!"

Glancing over her shoulder, she saw that Reece was fast gaining on her. She hesitated a fraction of a second, then pushed on. All she wanted was to find Princess, to escape from Reece and Vulture's Creek and the cabin that held his secrets. She knew that if she could just make it back to the inn, to the sanctuary of her room, she would survive with her sanity intact.

"Callie, wait!"

She tried to stay ahead of him, but then his hand caught her arm and he spun her around. He looked drenched and thoroughly miserable. His eyes reflected the darkness of the sky.

He dropped his hand, but he brought his face close to hers. "It's too late." His breath came in gulps. "You can't go that way, Callie. We've got to climb the hill."

Suddenly her anger flared, and she got a second wind. "No!" she snapped. "I'll do what I want to do. You can climb the hill without me."

"Callie, please . . . trust me."

He held out his hand again but didn't make a move to touch her.

"Why should I trust you, *Dr. Kenton Rhodes?*"

"Because in your heart you know that I love you," he shouted over the sound of the storm, "and that I wouldn't do anything to hurt you."

She raised her chin defiantly. Then just as quickly her resolve crumbled, and she was on the verge of tears.

All at once a great roar like a freight train rose above the moaning of the wind and the thunder. Callie gave a startled gasp and made a grab for Reece's hand. The next thing she knew, he was lifting her in his arms, carrying her.

The horrible noise grew in intensity until the ground shook, and Callie believed she would either go deaf or die from terror. She realized then what was happening. Years ago half the town of Vulture's Creek had been buried by a mud slide. Now history was repeating itself.

Reece began to run. She pressed her cheek against the shell of his jacket and clutched the wet fabric in her fingers. Once she looked up at his face; his eyes were fixed straight ahead, his features contorted in an expression of intense concentration. When they reached a rock ridge, he set her down.

The boarded-over mine shaft leaned into the hill like an old, dark ghost from where Callie stood. She looked toward Vulture's Creek and shuddered at the sight of a raging river of mud pummeling its way past the Silver Lode and the livery. The churning silt carried with it large rocks and uprooted trees. The pungent smell of wet earth nauseated her.

"Princess!" she cried, imagining the mare being helplessly swept up in the mud and water.

"Princess is fine," Reece shouted over a boom of thunder. "I found her, moved her to higher ground along with Moonfire. Now climb!" he ordered next to her ear. He grasped hold of her waist and gave her a push.

Callie scrabbled to gain her footing on the slick, rock-strewn hill. Time and again she felt herself slipping backward, but always Reece was there, right behind her, urging her forward with shouts of encouragement.

"To the left," he yelled at the moment she was certain she couldn't go on, "there's a shallow cave on a ledge. We'll wait out the storm there."

Callie was ready to drop from fatigue when Reece moved ahead of her. He took her hand in his and pulled her along to the opening of the cave.

They collapsed in a heap on the damp stone floor. For a

moment they lay side by side too tired to move. As her exhaustion slowly began to ebb, Callie became aware of his warm breath near her cheek. A violent chill suddenly shook her from head to toe.

"You're freezing," Reece whispered. He stroked back strands of wet hair from her brow. Then he sat up, bringing her with him. He stripped off his jacket, took something from an inner pocket, and wrapped the jacket around her shoulders and arms.

"The jacket's dry inside," she said through chattering teeth.

"It's got a waterproof lining." He took her hands between his and began to knead her fingers, coaxing the circulation back into them. "Your hands got pretty scraped up on the rocks."

She looked at her palms which had a network of scratches and cuts. She watched while Reece took a piece of white cloth from his jeans pocket and mopped up the bright beads of blood.

"Cloth's clean," he said. "Or was clean," he said with a slight smile. "We'll disinfect the cuts when we get back to the house, put a little antibiotic ointment on them."

Suddenly she was reminded of who he really was, what he was. "I guess you'd know about that, since you're a doctor," she said. She glanced away, but not before she saw the wounded look in his eyes. The brightening of the sky outside the cave seemed to her a cruel contrast to the misery-laden silence enveloping the dank, musty atmosphere inside.

Finally Reece got up and paced the few steps to the high, wide entrance. "Sun'll be out soon," he said.

Callie drew her knees up to her chin and hugged them. It was so strange, ironic. When she'd first seen Reece's sculptures in full sunlight, she'd had the eerie sensation that once they had been human too, and that if she stayed in the Sonoran Desert long enough, she might become one of them. She felt like a statue now—as cold and hard as stone.

Exhaustion overwhelmed her again; she couldn't imagine how she would ever find the strength to stand up, let alone walk under her own power back to wherever the horses were waiting.

As if he'd read her mind, he held out his hand to her; after a second's hesitation, she accepted it.

"Over here," he said, "where the light's better. There's something you have to read."

She took the two folded pieces of paper he gave her. At once she saw they were yellowed newspaper clippings. A headline in bold print seemed to leap out at her as she held one of the clippings up to the light.

Community Hospital Physician to Testify as Giardi Murder Trial Enters Fifth Week.

Callie read on silently.

Community Hospital internist Kenton C. Rhodes will take the witness stand for the prosecution when the trial of John J. Giardi, head of the local United Federation of Teamsters and with alleged ties to organized crime, resumes on Monday. Giardi stands accused of the ambush-style slaying of recognized crime boss Salvatore Ravoli in the Edwards Street parking garage. The alleged murder took place on the night of March 15th of last year. Also found dead at the scene was Marcus C. Miller, a local carpenter. Miller had just left his expectant wife, who was in labor, at the hospital's emergency room. Miller was apparently caught in the cross fire as he emerged from his car on the fourth floor of the garage.

Callie's lips and hands trembled as she looked up at Reece. "Where was this?"

"Pittsburgh." He bowed his head. "An innocent man was killed that night, Callie."

"And you saw it."

He pushed a wet lock of hair off his brow. "I was coming from a double shift at the hospital, bone-tired and anxious to get home to a warm bed and Anna Beth. I remember the time to the minute because I'd just checked my watch. One thirty-four A.M. and bitterly cold. I heard a man shouting, angry voices. I thought it was a gang fight—there'd been a couple of turf wars in the area, even a knifing. So I ducked behind a row of cars and crouched down in the shadows where I couldn't be seen."

Staring out at the sky, he went on. "Mary Miller delivered a baby girl that night, while her husband lay bleeding to death less than a quarter of a mile away." He gave a short, bitter laugh. "Here I was, a doctor, and I couldn't help him . . . couldn't save him. Can you imagine how that feels?" he whispered.

Her heart was breaking for him. "Reece, I—" She began to reach out to him, to tell him how sorry she was for ever doubting him. Then, sensing there was more he needed to say, she let her hand fall to her side and dug her nails into the flesh of her palm.

"Please . . . read the other article," he said.

Through a blur of tears, she learned from the headline and a few paragraphs underneath that John J. Giardi had been sentenced to death in the electric chair on one count of first-degree murder. She also learned that Kenton Rhodes's testimony had corroborated evidence presented by one of Giardi's accomplices, who had turned state's evidence, and that it was Rhodes's testimony that had convinced the jury to return a unanimous guilty verdict.

"After I came forward to the police, there were threats on my life, on Anna Beth's and her family's lives," he said when she was finished reading. "When I'd completed my testimony, I was put in the Witness Protection Program, given a new identity. Kenton Rhodes died the day Reece Tanner was born."

"But your wife . . . didn't she—"

"Anna Beth came from a large family. They were close-knit. From the first, she was opposed to my going to the police. She couldn't handle it, not when she saw what lay down the road, that it could mean giving up everything we'd worked so hard for . . . hoped for." His hands clenched at his sides. "Not when it meant she might never see her family again. She asked for a divorce before the trial began. Not too long after, she married some guy she'd known at work."

"Why did you go through with it, if you realized it meant she would leave you?"

"There was a picture in the paper of Mary Miller holding the new baby in her arms," he said in a voice raw with hurt. "Then she was on the news, crying, pleading that her husband's murderer be brought to justice." He passed a hand over his eyes. "The Millers had two other kids—a boy, nine, and a girl, seven. Sweet-looking kids. When I saw her . . . saw their pictures, I thought of the family Anna Beth and I had planned to start soon. How could I have lived with myself if I hadn't come forward and tried to help convict a thug who'd murdered an innocent man?"

Callie suddenly realized that his reply was what she would have expected him to say, what she had wanted him to say.

" 'War—killing of any sort—is a terrible thing,' " she murmured. " 'So many lives ruined, families torn apart—' "

He gazed at her, sorrow etching his handsome features.

"Those were Elena's words, not mine," she said. "I don't think I fully appreciated the truthfulness of them until now." She wiped the tears from her eyes. "How did you cope after . . . after it was over?"

He seemed to weigh the question. "Under the Witness Protection Program, I was set up with a job at the inn. I found Vulture's Creek and the cabin and spent weekends there for a couple of years with a few six-packs of beer and my grief for company. I guess you'd say that I was pretty paranoid for a while. I'd dream that Giardi had broken out of prison and that he and his thugs were on their way to get me. I'd wake up in a cold sweat, shaking, convinced Giardi was standing beside my bed with a gun aimed straight at my heart. Some nights I'd dream of Anna Beth.'' He sighed. ''Those were the nights when I almost wished Giardi would come after me to put me out of my misery.''

His shoulders sagged. ''When I found that loose stone in the fireplace, I figured it was as safe a spot as any to hide my memories. I wasn't supposed to keep those photos, the letters. But somehow I couldn't bring myself to get rid of them. They were my only link to the past, my reason for coming here in the first place. Finally I boarded over the windows and doors of the cabin, with the notion that I could still go back whenever I felt the need.''

''When I found the box, I thought it might belong to the vagrant you found in the mine.''

Reece shook his head. ''I don't suppose we'll ever know who he is.''

''What you told me about your parents—''

''Mostly a story. Both my parents are dead. They were never divorced. They had a terrific marriage.''

''Your brother who died of leukemia—''

''I don't have a brother. Or a sister. I guess that's why I placed so much importance on having kids of my own someday.'' He glanced at her. Holding his hands out in front of him, he continued, ''My father was a pediatrician, and real proud of the fact that I planned on being a doctor too. I wonder what he'd think if he knew that about the only thing these hands are good for now is chiseling a bunch of statues. I wonder what he'd think if he knew these hands will never be used to heal anyone again.''

''I know what he'd think,'' Callie said softly. ''He'd be even more proud of you now. But you're wrong about your hands.'' She took them in her own. ''They still have the power to heal.'' She brought them to her lips and placed a kiss on the smooth knuckles of each hand. ''They took care of my blisters, but more important, the strength and comfort of their touch healed me here.'' She brought them to rest over her heart and gazed into his eyes. ''I fell in love with a man named Reece Tanner, and he's the man I will always love.''

With a groan, he held out his arms to her, and she went into the safe harbor of his embrace. ''I love you, Callie,'' he whispered into her hair. ''With all my heart, I love you.''

''Forgive my thinking, for ever doubting...'' She rubbed her palms over his back, reveling in the pure joy of his nearness.

They stood locked in each other's arms for a time. Then he grasped her by the hand and led her out of the cave. ''Look,'' he said.

She stared down at the battered remnants of Vulture's Creek. All but a couple of the old buildings had been washed away or lay mired to their roofs in silt. ''The cabin—''

''It's gone.''

''And the box . . . your memories—''

''Gone too, buried where they belong.'' He took the yellowed newspaper clippings and tore them into shreds.

Callie watched as the breeze lifted the tiny pieces of paper from his hands and carried them heavenward. ''You told me once,'' she said, ''that the past is gone, that all we have is the present. You're right.''

''No, I was wrong.'' He took her into his arms. ''We have more than the present. We have forever, Callie.''

She laced her hands behind his back. ''To dance under the stars to the 'Sonoran Love Song'?''

''Every night.'' His hold on her tightened. ''We'll make our own memories. Say you'll marry me.''

She glanced at the sky, scoured clean once more and warmed by the sun. Then she gazed into Reece's eyes and saw the sun's warmth reflected there.

''Yes, I'll marry you,'' she said, giving herself up to the passion of his kiss, secure in the knowledge that this time her promise was for keeps.